ESCAPE

THE SEAM TRAVELERS BOOK ONE

Ray Wenck and Jason J. Nugent

Copyright © 2019 by Ray Wenck and Jason J. Nugent

All rights reserved. No part of this publication may be reproduced, distributed or transmitted in any form or by any means, without prior written permission.

Ray Wenck
raywenck.com

Jason J. Nugent
jasonjnugent.com

Publisher's Note: This is a work of fiction. Names, characters, places, and incidents are a product of the author's imagination. Locales and public names are sometimes used for atmospheric purposes. Any resemblance to actual people, living or dead, or to businesses, companies, events, institutions, or locales is completely coincidental.

Book Layout © 2016 BookDesignTemplates.com

Escape: The Seam Travelers Book One/ Ray Wenck and Jason J. Nugent. — 1st ed.

ISBN: 978-1090485847

Dedication

Dedicated to Terry, Molly and Angela for loving my kids despite their crazy dad.
-Ray

I'd like to dedicate this to my readers.
It's been awhile. I hope you enjoy!
-Jason

CHAPTER

One

Phetrix raced through the dark stone halls of the castle, his gray woolen robe trailing behind him. The invasion from the usurper Mortas Frost had begun and his duties to the prince and princess were paramount. They must be saved at all costs.

Shouting men in black armor and dying soldiers surrounded the castle. Flaming arrows streaked the sky and landed inside the castle, striking royal soldiers and igniting wood and clothing. Shouts for medical aid were called to Phetrix, but he ignored them. It pained him to let the injured go unattended. His obligation was to the children. If Mortas Frost gained access to the castle, all hope was gone.

Phetrix slipped on the cold stone floor when he turned a corner, his sandals losing traction in the fray, and nearly slammed into the wall. He righted himself and hurried to the nursery at the end of the hall.

"Are they safe?" he asked the guard stationed outside. He was a large barrel chested man named Wibar. Standing stoic with a sword at his belt and the white stag of King Artus on his armor, he dared anyone to cross him.

"Aye, they're safe. None have come through here but you. Come, inside quick."

He opened the large wooden door to a room decorated in bright paintings of mythical animals. Unicorns and dragons adorned the paintings, most crude interpretations colored by the children Erthic and Elysande, the two-year old twins of King Artus and Queen Gresilda.

"Erthic. Elysande," he said breathless, "Come. We need to go."

Elysande pouted. "No." She turned her back to him, facing an image of a griffon.

"You'll have time for disagreements later. We leave, now."

"No."

Erthic smiled, ready to join the fun. "No," he mimicked.

"We don't have time for this." Phetrix snatched each child into his arms and hurried out the door.

"Wibar, come. I will need your assistance. We must make sure the children are safe."

"I'm yours, mage. Nothing will happen to them as long as I live."

Phetrix entered the hall with the children in his arms and Wibar behind him.

Elysande squirmed and kicked.

"Cut that out! If you—"

She dropped from Phetrix's arms and ran, hurrying for the hallway ahead.

"Come back! Elysande! Don't run!"

He and Wibar ran after her, Erthic giggling at his sister's escape.

By the time they reached the intersection, she was gone. "Elysande! Where are you? This isn't a game! You're in danger!"

The girl giggled and stepped out from an open door

on the right. She stuck her tongue out at him and ran back in the room.

"Infernal girl! Come back here now!" He marched toward the door and turning inside, found her with one of Mortas Frost's men, the large white snowflake adorning his black armor giving him away.

"Let her go!" he demanded.

"Ely!" Erthic said, twisting in Phetrix's arms.

The mage set him down. "Stay behind me, do you understand?" The boy nodded.

"I'll be taking him, too," the soldier said. "Mortas will pay dearly for these two."

"He will get no satisfaction. They're under my protection. Touch one hair on her head and I will kill you."

The soldier laughed. "You? Kill me? With what? Wave of your hand and a magic word?" He ran a gauntleted hand through the girl's hair.

"Touch her and die," Wibar said, stepping out from behind the mage with his sword drawn.

"I warned you!" Phetrix said. The mage circled his hands in the air as though kneading dough and a bright ball of light appeared. He pushed it forward, enveloping the man's face.

"Stop that! I can't see!" he screamed. He uselessly fought the light.

"Elysande, hurry! Come quick!" The girl ran to him. "That's it, let's go before the spells wears off." She'd started crying and he held her close. "Wibar, finish this man."

The guard stepped around Phetrix and thrust his sword forward into the man's neck. He howled in agony, clutching at the sword, then let go and fell to the floor, his blood spreading out around him. Wibar wiped his sword on his trousers.

"He won't be bothering anyone again," Wibar muttered. Phetrix turned from the dying man, forcing the children to look away.

"Erthic, follow me! Stay close and don't linger!"

Smoke filled the corridors as Phetrix led them, grumbling about the prophecy. The tapestries on the walls were obscured by the increasingly heavy smoke. The children fell into a fit of coughing.

"I'm so sorry. We'll be out of this soon," Phetrix said. He placed a hand over Elysande's mouth, hoping to shield her from the smoke. She and her brother needed to survive at all costs.

Shouts ahead announced danger.

"There they are! Grab 'em before they escape!"

Wibar shoved them aside to get in front, and reached for his sword.

Black armored men with the snowflake of Mortas rushed them.

Wibar rushed forward, slicing down with his sword. "For the King and the children!"

He caught one enemy in the arm, but his armor protected him enough to deflect much of the blow. Wibar's weight in the blow made him stagger and one of the other soldiers rammed a dagger into his back. The large royal guard cried out, then the rest of the enemy soldiers were on him, swords and daggers piercing him mercilessly.

The children wailed but it was too late for Phetrix to help the man.

Reaching inside at the power he held, Phetrix created another, larger ball of light, and forced it toward the men. They shrieked in horror as the light approached and touched them.

"By the gods," Phetrix whispered. The men were engulfed in a fiery death, the intense heat from the light incinerating them as it moved forward until it dissipated leaving charred remains of four soldiers and Wibar smoldering on the ground.

Both children were hysterical, crying and barely able to control their emotions.

"Dead?" Elysande asked, the word difficult to hear in the chaos of the attack.

"Gone," Erthic said.

"No time. Come children," Phetrix said, carefully stepping through the blackened bones and burnt flesh. He approached another intersection and on both ends of the hall, black armored enemy soldiers faced him. They were trapped.

Nordon, the king's armorer, stepped into the hallway from a door midway between Phetrix and the enemy soldiers on the right, a massive warhammer held tight in his hands. Phetrix noticed a girl in the room where he came from, cowering and shaking.

"Nordon! Hold them off. I need a moment," Phetrix said. The large man nodded and grinned as he turned to the soldiers on their right.

"Let's do this," he growled. He raced toward them, swinging his mighty hammer with a deadly force. The sound of men screaming in agony and the hammer crashing through armor followed. The hall was filled with men and Phetrix didn't know if Nordon was winning or dying. All he knew was that it gave him the time to create the seam.

Samuel, I hope you're ready, Phetrix thought. He closed his eyes and focused. Men were dying around him. The serving girl was crying in the room. The children clung to him.

Phetrix reached deep within himself and conjured the spell he never imagined he'd ever have to use again. It was always a last resort if the castle was ever attacked. It was one of the few places he could perform such a feat.

When he opened his eyes, the hallway shimmered and distorted. It was like looking through water in a glass. Then sound quieted and motion slowed. He saw Nordon finish the men at his end of the corridor before he turned to run back toward the children. The enemy soldiers on the other side approached slowly, their way obstructed by Phetrix's powerful spell. Blood ran down Nordon's arm and his armor was stained with it.

Phetrix pushed harder and the distortion grew worse.

Nordon slowed, lowering his bloody hammer.

"It's our way out!" Phetrix called, noticing the large man's hesitation. "Hurry, I can let you pass. Bring the girl!"

Nordon's eyes widened.

"Now!" Phetrix yelled.

Nordon obeyed. He slid the warhammer into its sheath on his back and lifted the girl from the room, setting her down in the hallway. "This way Nadina," he said holding out a hand to pull her toward him.

Phetrix grew anxious. "If I don't make it, I need your oath Nordon. Swear to protect them. They cannot be found and if they are, they must be protected. The prophecy depends on it. Swear it!"

Nordon cocked his head to the side in deep thought then finally replied, "I swear."

"Hurry into the light, it won't hold for long."

Nadina timidly stepped forward near the bright slash of light.

"Go with her," Phetrix said to the children. Erthic grabbed her hand, Elysande stood next to her.

"Go through. The mage Samuel will guide you. I wish you the best. We will meet again."

Erthic walked with Nadina into the blinding light followed by Nordon. *Where was Elysande?* He thought.

"Ely! Where are you girl?"

The enemy soldiers were closing in, two of them entering the light.

"No!" He screamed. He had to close the seam. The boy would have to be safe with Nordon and Nadina.

He'd find the girl.

Phetrix waved his hands and the light vanished, leaving a faint echo in the dark corridor before winking out.

May the gods save you boy, he thought. He hurried away while the remaining enemy soldiers were disoriented. He had to find the girl before Mortas.

CHAPTER

Two

The attack on the castle lasted well into the night as did Phetrix's search for Elysande. If Mortas abducted her, or worse, killed her, their world was in trouble. At least he saved the boy. Saving one of them might have to be good enough.

Mortas Frost intended on plunging the kingdom into darkness and terror. Murdering the royal family was his only way to secure the outcome.

When Phetrix was younger, he served Mortas faithfully for close to ten years. The man was a monster.

Once, when they were on the march against King Artus's uncle Prince Willem, their army descended on a small village called Whispercross.

"Plunder all you want, kill any who oppose you. Do what you will with the women. We aren't staying long and none of them must be left alive," Mortas commanded them. Phetrix was in horror when he witnessed the brutal slaying of a young boy by one of the soldiers, all because he tried to save his sister.

That was when he realized the evil Mortas had become.

He knew the man was loose with his morals, but this was too much. While on the march toward Prince Willem's castle, Phetrix used a spell known to only a few of the most powerful mage's of the order and created a traveling tunnel to escape the terror. When he did, he stumbled onto something far more important.

Phetrix entered the tunnel, an immense blinding light that tore a seam in the fabric of time and space, but instead of finding himself closer to Willem's castle, he entered a world he'd never seen before.

Mechanical chariots, impossibly high buildings, and noise greeted him. He stood between two tall buildings with more glass windows than he'd ever seen in his life. People walked past him wearing odd clothing and unusual footwear and they stared at him, pointing and insulting him.

"By the gods! Another lives!" a man said to him. Phetrix was too stunned to reply. The man had come from one of the tall buildings.

"Come quickly! Are there more of you? Have you brought the king or Mortas?"

The man grabbed Phetrix by the hand and led him to one of the large buildings. They entered a door made of material he thought was metal. The man ushered him inside and led him to another door which opened to a small room.

Furniture unlike anything he'd ever seen before lined the walls. A box on a table caught his attention. Moving pictures flashed across the box, the sound screeching through it.

"What kind of sorcery is this?" Phetrix asked, pointing a long boney finger at the box.

"I have too little time to explain. I'm Samuel, faithful servant of King Artus."

Phetrix nearly fell over. "You're who?" He knew the name, the entire Order knew who he was.

"I thought you were dead? I was told you disappeared on the battle field."

Samuel nodded. "In a way, yes. I performed the same spell you did. It brought me here," he said waving his hands.

"Where is here?"

"Another dimension. Another world we never knew existed."

"But . . . I don't understand."

"It's not for us to understand, but to embrace. When King Artus learned of this, he instructed me to silence. He feared Mortas would push his evil across our land and he'd need an escape."

"Mortas?" Phetrix asked.

"Now I ask you again. Do you serve King Artus or Mortas?" Phetrix realized the man held a large dagger ready to strike.

"I serve--" He wasn't sure how to answer. He *had* been with Mortas, but the only reason he was here was because he'd fled the evil Mortas had become.

"I am Phetrix. I serve King Artus."

Samuel sheathed the dagger. "By the gods! We will survive this after all! Come, there is much to teach you."

Samuel went into the kitchen, banging items together. Once he was done, he produced two mugs of a dark liquid. "Have a seat Phetrix," he said nodding toward a table. Phetrix, still overwhelmed by his new surroundings, slowly approached the table and sat. Samuel handed him the mug, its warmth radiating outward.

"What is this?"

Samuel smiled. "They call it coffee. You'll like it."

Phetrix waited, wary it was a trap.

"It's fine, I promise." Samuel took the mug, sipped, and handed it back.

Expecting the man to get ill, Phetrix watched him carefully as he spoke.

"We are in a different world, a city they call Chicago. It's in a land called Illinois. Quite a loud place too." Samuel sipped from his own mug and continued.

"When you crossed the seam, you triggered an alarm. You tripped a spell really. It alerted me to the presence of one like me crossing the seam from our world to this one."

"Are you mad?" Phetrix whispered. Samuel chuckled.

"Mad? No. Cautious and prepared? Yes. I had no idea if that no good Rhoden Noster would discover the spell to cross the seam and I had to know whoever was coming across was friend or foe."

"How do you know I'm not an enemy? What makes you so sure I'm on your side?"

Samuel leaned in close. "Are you? On my side? On the side of King Artus? If you plan on returning home anytime soon, you'd do well to tell me the truth."

Phetrix sipped his drink, intent on showing Samuel he trusted him and he meant what he said about serving the King. "I was in the service of Mortas. I thought he was an honorable man. Until . . ." he trailed off, the memory of the looted village fresh in his mind, "Until he ordered a despicable act upon innocent people. I was awakened from my stupor and sought my way out."

Samuel leaned back. "So. You served Mortas," he said slowly, "but yet you claim allegiance to the King."

"King Artus is the rightful heir, I know that now. I've studied in the Order for years. I understand what's at stake."

"Then you know why it's paramount we preserve the King and his heirs."

"I do."

Samuel emptied his cup, went into the kitchen to refill it and sat back down. "A day," he said as he settled in.

"Excuse me?"

"A day. Give me a day where I can show you this world and I'll show you how to get back to ours."

Phetrix considered his request. "Fine. A day. Then I'd like to get back home."

"In the morning, we'll go out and I'll show you around. Then I'll share how to get back. Tonight, you can sleep on the couch."

"The . . . couch?"

Samuel smiled and pointed in the other room. "That over there. I'll get you some clothes in the morning so you don't stand out like you do now."

Phetrix barely slept that night, worried if he was being set up by Samuel.

CHAPTER

Three

Phetrix awoke when Samuel dropped a pan in the kitchen.

"Sorry about that! Just getting some breakfast before we go out. I've got pants and a t-shirt on the chair over there. I guessed your size, I hope they work."

The white haired older man busied himself with the pan, swirling eggs and frying bacon, a scent Phetrix knew all too well from home. He changed into the clothes provided and stared at himself in a mirror he noticed in the bathroom. He wore dark blue pants that were thick. The shirt had the sigil of some local lord.

"What is this? What lord do you serve?" Phetrix asked pointing at his shirt. If he was going to be in public, he wanted to know what lord he was with. He couldn't be too careful.

Samuel laughed. "It's not a lord, it's a team. A baseball team to be exact. The Cubs."

"A . . . baseball team?"

"It's a sport in this world. In this city, the Cubs are one of their local teams."

"Oh." Phetrix let it go, figuring wearing the sigil of a team wasn't as bad as a rival lord.

After breakfast and more of the coffee drink, Samuel took Phetrix out to explore their surroundings.

Samuel tried his best to offer commentary as they walked. "Chicago is one of the largest cities in this country. It's in the center of the nation and has a busy airport, which may come in handy if we ever have to escape."

"An airport?"

"You see those," Samuel pointed upwards at a slow moving bird with white smoke trailing behind, "those are airplanes. They've figured out how to put people in the air. Quite a remarkable achievement if you ask me."

Phetrix stared at the airplane above, oblivious to the throngs of people walking past them.

"Come, we've got more to see." Samuel nudged him and they joined the flow of people.

"Just outside my apartment where I found you is one entry point to this world. There's another by a parking garage on the southside. Beyond that, I don't know of any other places where a seam can emerge."

"What's a parking garage?"

"Do you see where those cars are going over there, that's a parking garage. Think of it like a . . ." he paused then lit up as the analogy occurred to him, "think of it like a stable for these wheeled chariots they call cars."

Phetrix nodded his understanding. To be honest, the sounds, sights, and the constant smell of something like the lavatories back home overwhelmed him.

"Why are you here Samuel? Why not try to work back in Chevalon? Wouldn't you be more helpful there?"

The older mage turned to him. "There are too many who know me or about me back home. Mortas has been after me, hoping to force me into his service like he's done with Rhoden. Since I refused, he wants me dead. Did you know Rhoden was a student of mine? He's more powerful than you can imagine. Do not underestimate him. Ever!" Samuel punctuated his words with a finger to Phetrix's chest.

They walked around the busy city for hours, Samuel droning on about something called pizza and beers, though Phetrix never saw any. Finally, he'd had enough.

"Samuel, I appreciate the tour, but this is all too much for me. How did this world exist without us ever knowing? What does this have to do with the King and his heirs?"

Samuel stopped, his eyes darting back and forth, then he spoke in a quiet voice. "If Mortas ever comes for the heirs, they'll be safe here. We can protect them within the confines of this city. They'd be anonymous here. No one knows how to travel the seam other than you and I. We need to keep it that way."

Phetrix wondered about the viability of leaving their world to remain in this one, but Samuel seemed convinced. He didn't bother to try and change his mind. King Artus was in no real danger, no matter how much Mortas harassed his smaller lieges. Mortas was wicked, but he didn't seem to have the resources to carry out his overthrow.

"Say, where were you when you travelled the seam? There were only two places I knew of that opened to this world."

Phetrix closed his eyes and recalled where was the moment he opened the seam. "I was near Whispercross."

"Whispercross? That little village? I'd never have found that!"

"I fled Mortas and his army, opening the seam right there. I had no idea it was dependent on a particular place. I just used the spell and found myself here."

Samuel's eyes widened and he spoke in hushed tones. "The location has everything to do with where you go. This is the third world I visited."

"What? No. How does that make sense?"

"Look around, Phetrix, none of this makes sense when you think about it. But yet, here we are. Remember Whispercross. That will get you back here. So will the King's castle."

Phetrix was confused.

"Don't worry. I discovered it long ago. It's quite handy if ever under attack." He winked and slapped Phetrix on the arm. "Come now, I assume you'll want to get back home."

They retraced their way, returning to the building where they started.

Phetrix was exhausted and slowly slipped back into his robes, the familiar feel comforting him.

Samuel led him to another room in the apartment. Inside it was dark. He lit several candles revealing walls covered in writing Phetrix recognized from spell books.

"Stand there," Samuel said pointing at a large X painted on the floor.

Phetrix did as he was told.

"When you return, visit the library in King Artus's castle. Hidden behind the potions books is a trap door where you'll find an exact copy of this spell. Learn it. If you ever return, you'll need it to get back. I might not be here next time. I've also listed the other locations to enter the seam."

Phetrix nodded, still unsure if this was all a dream or something worse.

Samuel opened a book and started reading the spell. Soon the room erupted in a brilliant white light that consumed Phetrix. He shielded his eyes to it and when he opened them, he stood outside the walls of the king's castle.

Before he'd sent Erthic to the realm, that was the only time he'd ever been there.

CHAPTER

Four

Samuel waited, his impatience showing in the form of his muttering and pacing. The three men with him, all former guards of the now deposed king, stood calmly awaiting his orders. Each man wore a dark suit and sunglasses, giving the appearance of being professional bodyguards. In fact, once Samuel figured out the new world, he had them all trained for this very purpose. They stood positioned to observe anyone approaching from any direction.

Samuel stopped his pacing and whirled on the eldest of the three guards, a one-time captain named Trenton. "Are you sure your source was reliable?" he asked for the fifth time since they'd taken up their vigil.

"Yes. He is reliable. The castle *is* under attack and *does* look like it has fallen."

Samuel eyed him, ready to snap at the man for his insolent tone. Instead, he pivoted and began pacing once more.

Samuel had also traded in his lavish robes for a tailored suit. The expensive wardrobe fitted his economic standing. He'd done well in this new world--well, not so new now. The discovery that his magic still worked had a lot to do with his success.

He reached the end of the unofficial path and pivoted for the return. *Where was Phetrix? Had he died in the battle?* He prayed not. If the mage fell, all was lost. If Phetrix was unable to get the King, Queen and the children out of danger then all hope of saving the kingdom was gone forever. Mortas Frost would rule until his death, which could never come soon enough for the people of the land. He was a brutal tyrant, who took pleasure in other's agony. He would make the people suffer greatly.

If the castle fell, the only chance they had of recovering it was if a member of the royal family survived the assault. However, even if they did, Mortas would hunt them endlessly until they were found, torturing and executing any he thought who might be harboring them. Oh, this was bad. So very bad.

A sudden sound caught his attention, like that of an electrical current followed by a tearing of heavy fabric. He spun to face the noise. The three guards took defensive stances all now holding guns.

A dark line appeared head high, stretching across the open air. The location of the seam was not ideal. When he'd first discovered the seam years before, it was in an alley that blocked the view of its strangeness. Since that time, one of the buildings had been demolished in a nuisance abatement sweep. Nothing had replaced the structure which left the seam open on one side. Though not many people walked this section of the city, a lot of cars passed. Anyone could see the seam, although not many would understand its purpose. However, if they spotted people appearing out of thin air, it might be another matter. Especially with the wide use of their communication devices.

A hand reached through pulling on the fabric of the

world and made it wider. Samuel and Trenton stepped closer as a toddler was lowered from the gap. Trenton took the terrified boy and handed him off to one of his men. Next came a young woman, equally as scared as the boy. Trenton took her around the waist and lowered her to the ground. The second guard came forward and ushered her to the side. Her face drained of all color as she scanned her new home. She fainted and the guard was forced to lift and carry her toward the waiting van.

The last figure through was a hulk of a man. He stepped through, but no amount of assistance would help him to the ground without causing injury to the assister. The man jumped down. He carried a large warhammer on his back. His massive arms made him appear like something out of the comic books the men were always reading.

"Quick, get them to the van," Samuel commanded.

The two guards took the new arrivals while Trenton and Samuel waited for others. When none came, Samuel levitated to the seam and peered through. The hallway was filled with smoke making it difficult to see. Then, a face came into focus. It was Phetrix. He felt his heart lighten, knowing the mage was still alive. They locked eyes for the briefest of moments. Samuels eyes asked the question, 'What about the King, Queen and the girl?' Phetrix shook his head and shrugged. The seam closed as if a zipper had been drawn. It winked out with an audible pop.

Samuel hovered above the ground lost in thought and sorrow. Were they only able to save one of the four? "This is bad," he said to himself.

Trenton stepped forward and placed a hand on

Samuel's arm. "Whether we're staying or leaving, you must not stand out to bystanders."

Samuel looked confused for a moment, then understood and lowered himself to the ground. he had to think. What needed to be done? He grabbed Trenton's arm. "If the boy is the only survivor we must protect him. No harm can come to him or all is lost. Leave one of your men with me and take the others to the house we bought for them. Tell the big man to help guard the boy. Let the woman take care of the boy. You stay with them. Send the other guard back with the van, but only once you're sure all is secure. Keep him safe, Trenton."

Trenton nodded and jogged to the van. One of the guards, Darden, he thought, he could never keep their names straight, shoved the side door shut and the van drove away. He then moved toward Samuel keeping his distance to better take in the surroundings.

Samuel looked around. He had to find someplace to watch from. Standing here for hours would draw attention and that was the last thing he needed. He walked toward the street. he didn't need to speak or motion to the guard. The man would follow. Protection was what he was trained to do and Darden was good at his job.

They walked across the street and entered a three-story parking garage. There, Samuel took up his stakeout. He prayed his vigil would bear fruit and Phetrix would find and deliver the rest of the royal family. He had been happy to discover Phetrix was still alive. However, now that he knew he only managed to save one of the four he was charged with protecting, Samuel cursed him.

How could he not have been prepared for this outcome? The man bungled the job. The only job he really had. He was happy his fellow mage was alive, but if the King, Queen and daughter were dead, the man had a lot to answer for.

CHAPTER

Five

The van returned two hours later carrying Trenton and the other guard, Mathu. It stopped and Trenton got out.

"Samuel, you should go. Get them set up. Explain what you need to and set the wards. I will stay here and keep watch. I'll call you if anything happens."

Samuel wanted to object, but Trenton's words made sense. Besides, if the boy was the only royal member to survive, it was important he got him secured as soon as possible. He nodded, got in the van and was lost in thought.

The drive was a good thirty minutes to the old residential neighborhood. He had purchased the house days before, paying cash at a well below market price. He chose the location because it was an established neighborhood, with residents who, for the most part stayed out of other people's business. He could have set them up in more luxurious quarters, but until they were familiar with their new world, he didn't want to risk them coming under scrutiny.

The house was a two-story, aluminum sided structure with a walk-up attic and full basement. It was within walking distance of stores, schools and a park. It was also less than a minute from an expressway in case the need for a quick escape arose.

Mathu pulled up to the curb in front of the house.

Samuel exited and climbed the stairs. Mathu followed eyeing the street as he went. Samuel knocked and after a bit of hesitation, the door was opened by the huge man. He held the heavy warhammer in one hand, ready to strike. Samuel had no doubt the man knew how to wield the weapon.

The woman and child sat on a sofa. She looked more anxious than the boy did. A little color had returned to her cheeks since she'd stepped into the new world. He studied them each for a moment, then said, "I am Samuel. I will be your contact here. If ever there is an emergency of any sort I am the only one you contact."

Her voice frail and shaking, the woman said, "You mean, you're going to leave us here alone?"

"You'll hardly be alone, dear girl. You will have each other. But, not to worry. I will not leave until I'm satisfied that you can survive and flourish here. You have so much to learn. There's so much to tell you, I barely know where to begin. It will be overwhelming at first, but you'll catch on."

"Are we to stay here, then, sir?"

"That's right. It wouldn't be safe for you to go back now. It appears as though Mortas Frost has taken control of the castle. That may mean this little man's family is no more. If that is the case, it is up to us to protect him until such a time as we can take our lands back."

Samuel sat in the rocking chair opposite the sofa. He would have asked the big man to sit as well, but he feared the sofa might not hold his weight.

"First of all, tell me your names."

"I," the big man put a fist to his chest in case Samuel didn't understand which I he was referring to, "am Nordon. I was the castle's blacksmith."

That explains the muscular arms, Samuel thought.

"My name is Nadina. I worked in the kitchen."

"And this little man is Erthic." He smiled at the lad, but the boy just stared at him, not comprehending everything.

"This is a modern world, full of all manner of people and strange ideas. This house alone has so many magical items as to be called a wizard's keep. It will take time to explain them. Some you will need to know while others you can learn for yourself.

"Let's start with the names. From now on, you are Don and, uh, Dina. We'll figure out a surname later. The boy will be known as. You are to pose as husband and wife. Eric is your son. Your primary function is to protect Eric at all times and at all costs.

"Nordon, you come with me. I need to show you the houses defenses. Mathu, why don't you take Dina into the kitchen and show her how things work."

Samuel rose and started for the stairs. Nordon followed, Dina stood and went after Mathu.

"Stop!" Samuel shouted. "You have already failed in your duty to the prince." His angry eyes swept from Dina to Don. "One of you must be with the prince at all times."

Dina shuffled to the sofa and scooped the boy up in her arms.

"Don't forget again," Samuel warned.

Over the next several hours and going deep into the night, Samuel gave explanations and lessons in the use of the various safeguards and features of the house. Most were modern technology, some were magical enhancements. All would take time for the two new residents to understand.

Late into the early morning, they took a break. Eric had been asleep for hours. Dina had drifted off an hour ago. Samuel could see the exhaustion drooping Nordon's face, but knew the big man would never complain. Samuel told him to catch some sleep and they would start again at sunrise.

Tired as well, Samuel could not sleep until he checked once more with Trenton. Still no sighting of the royal family. He sent Mathu to relieve the other two and went to sleep. He was up early. Darden was busy in the kitchen showing Dina how to use the stove. Twenty minutes later the entire household was seated at the dining room table having breakfast.

Samuel had just taken a bite of a piece of bacon when his phone rang. He dropped his fork with a clatter on the plate and snatched up his phone.

"What news?" He listened. Then said, "I'm on my way." He stood. "Nordon, you're in charge. Do not leave the house and don't let anyone in other than the people you've met here. Mathu, we need to go."

Mathu jammed three pieces of bacon into his mouth and rose. They hustled out the door and to the van. They arrived in record time. No sooner had the van pulled to the curb, then Trenton ran from the parking garage with a young girl in his arms. Deardon followed, his arm around a tall woman.

They hopped into the back of the van and Mathu had it moving before everyone had settled into a seat. Trenton handed the princess to the woman and pulled his weapon from the shoulder holster he wore.

Samuel said, "Is that it? No King or Queen?"

"No, sir. When they came through, Phetrix said, 'The castle is lost and the KIng and Queen have vanished.'"

Samuel sighed and faced the front. If the King and Queen had vanished, perhaps they escaped. There would be word if they had been captured by Mortas Frost. And everyone would know if they had been killed. Well, nothing they could do about it. They had the prince and princess. It was his job to make sure they survived and grew to an age where they could lead a rebellion.

"Take us to the second house. I don't want them living together."

He had much to do. He needed Id's for the kids and their guardians. They would need a crash course on survival skills for this world. He needed to set the magical wards that would keep them hidden from any who might follow and just so many more details. But he was good at details. It was one of the reasons he'd thrived in a world so beyond his imagination as to never have been a notion.

Samuel would see to everything and when they were ready, he would lead the prince and princess back to their world to reclaim the throne. It was only going to take time and that, thanks to the efforts of Phetrix, they now had.

CHAPTER

Six

Phetrix scoured the castle, losing hope of ever finding Elysande. He feared she might be dead. Dead royal soldiers lay in heaps at nearly every turn. Smoke wafted through the corridors. Mortas brought death in his wake and if that little girl was caught in it, Phetrix was prepared to cross the seam and share the word with Samuel himself. At least Erthic was safe, as far as he knew.

Phetrix turned a corner near the kitchens and listened as he thought he heard a faint sound.

"Ely? Ely is that you dear?" He drew on his power, ready to unleash it on any enemy soldier that might have the unfortunate distinction of harming the girl.

Shouting men from his left startled him, but they were too far off for the moment.

"Ely? Come out dear. It's me, Phetrix. I can take you to your brother." He waited, listening for the sound he heard moments earlier.

The shouting soldiers seemed to be closer, their voices carrying a touch of mirth. He slipped into the kitchen hoping to avoid detection, unsure how large a group was headed his way.

Hope waned.

Then, he heard it again and it was nearby.

Opening every cabinet and every scorched door, he moved silently throughout the kitchen. The place had been burnt in the attack the previous night and looted already. Pots and pans were tossed about the kitchen, a mess the cook would never have allowed to happen had she been there . . . and alive.

Then he found her.

He heard her crying softly and followed the sound to a slightly tilted cupboard door.

"My dear, I've found you!" he said when he opened the door to the hysterical child inside. "Come, I can save you yet." He reached his hand out to her and at first she slapped it away, then realizing who he was, she accepted it. "That's it Ely. Hurry, your brother awaits." She crawled out from the cupboard and clung to him.

The soldiers seemed to have passed as their voices carried toward him from the opposite direction he heard earlier. Carefully, they left the kitchen when they heard a woman's scream from another room.

"Quiet Ely, I need to check on this."

He considered leaving the girl, whoever it was, but her screams called to him. If she were in trouble, he had to do something. He left Mortas' service because of horrific actions like this. Now was the moment to act, even if it meant putting the princess in harm's way.

Channeling a small stream of power, Phetrix turned to Ely. "Stay here. Watch me, but stay here. Got it?" The girl crossed her arms and scowled. It would have to do.

Phetrix crept closer to the open door and peered inside to see a servant girl being fondled by one of Mortas' soldiers.

"Come on wench, stop yer fighting," the man said. Phetrix noticed the black armored man's sword in its scabbard still attached to his belt lying on the floor. His pants were around his ankles.

"Your gonna die soon anyway, so, why are ya giving me a hard time?"

That was enough. Phetrix let loose a tiny bolt of light. It was dark purple and bore through the soldier, melting a hole in his armor and coming out the other side. He turned to look at the hole now punched through him, and fell down on the girl. The servant screamed when the dead man fell on her.

She cried, thrashing until the lifeless man fell off her. That's when Phetrix realized who it was.

"Alyanna? Alyanna, you're safe!" he said.

"Phetrix?" she asked, wiping her eyes. "You have the princess!"

Elysande ran to her, a woman she'd known since birth.

"Alyanna, you've been around the children since early on, right?"

She nodded as she wiped at the tears on her face. The man had ripped her tunic and was trying to grope her when Phetrix came upon them. Fortunately he did, as it presented a new opportunity for him.

"I was their first nanny. I'm still one of many that help raise them." She squeezed Ely, her arms clinging tight to the girl. Watching Ely's face light up within Alyanna's grasp, he knew it could work.

"I don't have much time. The castle is in ruins and the King and Queen are missing. I need a favor." He wrung his hands. He was taking a massive risk with the child, but he had little recourse left. Erthic had already been sent through the seam and should be with Samuel by now. He had to send Ely through as well. It was the only way he could think of to save her.

"I need you to flee with her. Now." It wasn't ideal, but he trusted Alyanna and more importantly, so did Ely. He could only hope they connected with Samuel and eventually Erthic when they got to the other side. He had no time to train her in the ways of the new world and she'd have to cope with the massive change as best she could. It was far too late for a different plan.

Phetrix didn't wait for her reply, but instead spoke the words that created the seam. The white light illuminated the room.

"What is this?" Alyanna asked.

"Your salvation. It's the only way out. You'll never leave the castle alive if you don't go through. Mortas' men are everywhere. They searching for her," he said pointing at Ely, "and if what just happened to you by that solider is any indication, it is quite likely more will try and do the same. Mortas encourages that kind of behavior. You'll be safe. Take Elysande. Erthic is already there. He's with Nadron and Nadina. Find Samuel and live. Hurry, before more of them come."

Elyande tugged at Alyanna. "Brother," she said.

Men shouted in the corridor outside. "Hurry Belam! We want our turn with her too!"

"Go now!" Phetrix urged. Alyanna looked to the door and then to the light.

"But, I don't know—"

"Now!" Phetrix pleaded with her. Elysande held her hand tight, urging her forward. Then, the princess stepped through the light and Alyanna reluctantly followed.

CHAPTER

Seven

Mortas Frost sat atop a black steed overlooking the burning valley below. A wicked grin flashed across his face.

"Well done," he said to himself. "Well done indeed."

In the midst of the valley lay the remains of King Artus's castle. It would have been better to secure it instead of razing it, but he wanted the people to know who was now in charge.

Somehow, that mage Phetrix had whisked the children away, but they'd be found sooner or later. He'd dedicate as many resources as needed to find them. As long they lived, his reign would be threatened. And he wasn't accustomed to that.

A horse drew up behind him and a young soldier dropped from the saddle, kneeling on the ground. Mortas waved his hand upward for the man to stand.

"Sir, the royal family is missing. We've yet to find them."

Mortas' anger flared. He reared his horse, and the animal brought its hooves down inches from the frightened man's head.

"I will not tolerate incompetence. Locate the family and bring them to me. Failure to do so will not end well for you."

"Yes sir." On shaky legs, the soldier climbed back

atop his own horse and raced toward the main camp.

"They must be found at all costs. I cannot have them running around alive, offering hope when there is none to be had." He patted his horse and turned from the ledge, satisfied at the destruction below.

***

Several days passed and still no word on the family. Mortas had executed three soldiers who dared tell him the family could not be found. His patience was gone, replaced by an unending foul mood that had everyone scampering from his path. Further delays were not acceptable.

Mortas rested inside the massive tent in the center of the camp. His men were securing the kingdom and scouting for a suitable location to build his grand castle.

"Sir, your mage approaches," a guard at the tent door called inside.

"Good! I've had need of Rhoden Noster."

Mortas sat up and adjusted his shirt, buttoning it closed after his serving girl had unfastened it earlier. Rhoden pushed aside the tent flap.

"My liege, may I come in?"

"Rhoden! Come, come. It's been too long. What word do you bring?"

"I've come about the family."

"Of course you have. Please, have a seat." Mortas motioned to a small stool in the corner.

"Now. What about them?"

Rhoden fidgeted, intertwining his fingers together.

"Sir," he began, "I have interviewed both our soldiers and various members of King Artus' staff when they were taken prisoner. There was much smoke and confusion, but from the information I gathered, I have reason to believe Phetrix used a spell unknown to most like me. It's a spell only the most powerful can replicate."

"So? What's that got to do with anything?"

"Everything, sir. I believe he used it while in the castle to whisk away the children."

"To where? What proof do you have for this claim?" Mortas dragged a stool in front of Rhoden and sat, leaning closer with his hands on his knees.

"Where? I don't exactly know, sir. It's hard to explain. My old master Samuel knew of such powerful magic. It's called traveling magic. He tried to teach me once, but I got bored of his ramblings and never paid much attention. I preferred more aggressive forms of my art. But from what the soldiers described of the incident, I feel certain that's the spell Phetrix used."

"Well, what does it do?"

"It opens a portal, sir. A passageway to another world."

Mortas stood and circled around the tent. "Another world? What kind of nonsense are you speaking?"

"None, sir. It's a powerful spell known only by a select group of mage's. Most of them long dead.

"It is an ancient art form with its roots in the very creation of our world. At least that is what I've been told."

"What is this other world? Where is it? If he took the children there, we must track them and end this."

"I agree, sir. However—"

"However what?" Mortas growled.

"No mage known can do such a thing."

"You mean other than Phetrix?"

Rhoden hung his head. "Correct, sir. I know if I had the time, I'd be able to learn it. My powers are stronger than Phetrix's."

Mortas rushed to the mage and leaned in close, his finger pressing against his chest. "Do not fail me in this! Finding those children is paramount. Do you understand me?"

"Of course, sir. Your victory will be secure when we do. I realize the importance of this. I shall discover this spell and we will soon have the power to find them."

"I expect victory, Rhoden. Nothing less."

The mage stood, bowed, and left the tent. Mortas paced around the tent with his hands clasped behind his back.

They scoured the castle after taking it and there was no sign of the children or Phetrix. Artus and his nagging wife were missing as well. Most likely they were in hiding, though they'd never outlast his desire to seek them out. He hoped they'd be found alive so he could make a vivid example of them with a public execution. His hold on the kingdom would only be strengthened by it.

"One day, all of this will be mine. No one will dare oppose me, not when I rid this land of that foul family. Soon. Very soon my hold will be complete."

CHAPTER

Eight

Fifteen Years Later

With a simultaneous burst, they sat bolt upright in the bed, a mix of shock and fear playing across their faces.

"Oh, God!" she said. "They found us."

Intermittent amber lights flashed in their room. A magically enhanced alarm tone, unheard anywhere else in the house, beeped in frenzied repetition. After all this time, the enemy had found them.

"Check the monitors," the large, balding man said. "I'll see to the boy."

They started to move, but the man grabbed her arm and held tight. "Nadina," he said in a firm voice. "Remember our mission and your training."

Her face relaxed. The worry wrinkles along her forehead and temples, disappeared. As if by magic, a different woman gazed back. A look of control and power filled her now narrowed eyes. He gave a reassuring squeeze and let go. She nodded, rolled off the bed and disappeared beneath. When she reappeared, she held a short sword and an Uzi—a modern medieval warrior ready for battle. He stood and armed himself with a weapon large enough to need both hands to hold. However, his well-muscled arms held it outward in one steel-gripped fist.

He did not know the proper name for the massive

gun. It had been given to him years ago for just such a purpose. It shot 7.62 caliber rounds out of one barrel, shotgun shells out of another and an experimental, heat seeking grenade from a third. When asked questions about the weapon, the man who gave it to him said, "The bullets go in there, there and there and come out here, here and here. That's all you need to know."

He left the room and Dina raced toward the bedroom closet. She opened the door and shoved the hangers aside, revealing a second door. This one led to the walk-up attic. She entered and climbed the stairs. The attic featured an assortment of monitors, electronics, weapons and storage trunks.

She pushed a button on a console, shutting down the alarm, then examined the four small monitors. Each one showed dark, infrared images from the four directions of the house. At the moment, no pictures were displayed. Each screen showed only the empty, dark night.

A tiny red light pulsed on the monitor responsible for the alarm. Dina tapped a few keys on the portable board in front of that monitor and sent the picture to a larger, central screen. She leaned close, but no matter how hard she strained to see, no threat appeared. A few more key strokes and the pictures ran in reverse. She guessed at the amount of time passed since the alarm sounded, then switched to forward. The recorded scene began to play.

Two minutes later, the reason for the triggered alarm came into view. The sight unnerved her enough to seek the support of a chair. The ghostly image of a

Seeker floated past, ten feet above the roof lines of the neighborhood houses. "Oh, saints preserve us."

As she studied the image, her fingers caressed the gun like it was a support animal. She'd only heard of such things, being told stories in her youth but she always thought they were tales made up to scare children into good behavior. Now, she knew those tales were real. After fifteen years of peace, those who searched for them had found an opening into this world. Dina watched the replay through once, then rewound it and scanned again. The Seeker, part creature, part spirit, floated past without paying attention to their house. It would be tuned to the special frequency the boy emanated, but wards had been set to prevent that from happening. They appeared to be working, but wait. Was that a hesitation?

With nimble fingers, she reset the recording and ran it through again, then enhanced and enlarged the image and played it in slow motion. Yes, right there. The Seeker turned its horrendous head toward the house, pausing for just an instant in its methodical side-to-side sweep. Whatever it felt had not been sufficient to warrant a closer look, but it had sensed something. Samuel, the contact for this world, had to be notified. The enemy had entered this world and was actively searching for the ward they had been entrusted to protect.

Dina set the weapons down and reached for the dedicated encrypted radio, surprised to find her hand shook. She pulled it back, cupped it in the other hand and said a quick prayer to buoy her courage. She did not have to dial, punch in, or speak a number. Once the headset was lifted from its cradle, the call was activated.

A voice on the other end, said, "Yes?"

"They're here."

Silence weighed heavy on the other end. "You know what to do. I'll be in touch." The disconnect had an eerie finality to it. Dina set the handset down gently, released the breath she'd been unaware she held, and got up.

Downstairs she found Nordon, in front of the boy's bedroom door, a lethal protector, ready to give his life for his charge. He tensed when she appeared, an unspoken question in the one lifted eyebrow. She nodded. Her body deflated. She leaned forward, placing her head against his massive chest. "Oh, Nordon, what are we going to do?"

"What we were trained for." He put an arm around her to comfort her as well as himself. "What we were trained for, my love," he repeated. "And may the Gods be with us."

She added, "I hope they can find us in this strange world we now call home."

CHAPTER

Nine

Nadina watched Eric through the front picture window as he raked the leaves that had fallen from the tree in the front yard. A cup of steaming coffee was held firmly between her still trembling hands. The poor boy had no idea the dangers that now lurked, searching for him. But he also had no idea who he really was.

Nordon had left early in the morning before Eric had risen, to meet with Samuel. She hoped he came back with a plan that allowed them to continue their lives in peace. She paused the cup inches from her lips as an alternate thought came to her. She hoped he had a plan that allowed them to continue living, period.

Eric was a good boy. They raised him as a mission initially, but along the way, fell in love with him as if he were their own. He seldom gave them trouble of any sort. He did his chores with no complaint, was a stellar student and amazing athlete, even if he wasn't allowed to participate in any sports at school.

He was tall, and though slender, had a strong toned frame that promised to fill out in a most alluring way. His handsome features, dark-blonde hair, and brilliant smile drew much attention from the girls at school, as well as the local MILFs and cougars. He was a splendid male specimen who had a great life ahead of him, providing he lived long enough to realize it.

She consummated her sip, the taste, warmth and aroma invigorating her. She remembered the first time she'd been introduced to the then, vile liquid. It was bitter and strong and made her stomach heave. Now, she could barely function without at least two cups of the beverage each morning.

It was amazing what she learned to enjoy over the past fifteen years. Fifteen. Had it really been that long since Nordon and her were thrust into this new world and given the task of protecting Eric, then known as Erthic? She was but a girl herself, unmarried, naive and frightened. But the mage found her in the lower chambers and forced a pledge of protection from her. Then, he'd pushed her through an opening between worlds with the then three year old boy and a man she'd never met, and had entrusted her with the future of their world. My God, how far they'd come.

Samuel found them and set them up as Don And Dina. Nordon and her were forced to live together, complete strangers, in a strange place that moved much faster than either of them thought possible. In those first few months, they barely left the house for fear of having to interact with the people.

Eric piled the leaves, then moved on to rake another area of the lawn. He wiped his sweat coated forehead on a sleeve and caught sight of her standing in the window. He smiled, waved and went back to his task.

She waved back even though he was no longer watching. Warmth spread through her in a far superior and more intense form than the coffee ever could. He might not be hers, and perhaps she'd never have any of her own, but she did love him deeply and that love was enough for her to lay down her life to protect him.

With that thought in mind, she climbed the stairs to check the monitors again, praying she would never see a threat of any sort. The monitors were clear, the wards silent. Loathe to leave Eric out of sight for too long, she tucked a handgun into her slacks at her back and lowered the heavy sweatshirt over the weapon. Though warm for this time of year, the constant bone chilling iciness she felt made the sweatshirt necessary and not just to cover the gun.

Downstairs, she took a look out the front window to make sure Eric was still there, then refilled her mug and sat on the front porch. As she watched him work, a warmth spread from her core melting her chill if only for the moment.

Eric hummed. His body perspired from the effort, but the work wasn't strenuous. He enjoyed toiling outdoors. He stopped for a minute and closed his eyes as a slight breeze against his damp skin seemed to invigorate him. The wind lifted his hair from his head and dropped it back out of place. He ran a hand down it's length to plaster it to his head.

He finished another pile of leaves and started on the last section of lawn. From across the street, Madeline, the cute and curious three year old, who lived in the two-story house two down on the opposite side, called out.

"Hi Reric."

She couldn't quite say his name. Her long brown curls bounced as she walked and waved.

He smiled and waved back. "Good morning, Madeline. How are you today?"

"I'm good," she said in a sing-song voice.

She turned down the apron of the driveway directly across the street. Eric shot nervous glances down both directions of the street. Dina fired one toward Madeline's house looking for her mother. Sissy was a nice girl, but she was only a few years older than Eric. Addicted to her cell phone, she often lost track of Madeline. She felt sorry for Madeline, knowing she was left on her own to entertain herself much too often and for way too long. Dina also worried, since she wandered the neighborhood on her own on a daily basis.

They lived in an older area of town called the North End. The streets were lined end to end with one and two story homes built in the early to mid nineteen hundreds. They had little street frontage and were set close to the road. Cars were parked on each side of the street forcing traffic down to one lane—a problem when cars came from opposite directions at the same time.

It was not a poor neighborhood, but at the same time, it was a long way from being a wealthy one. Most of the properties were well kept and turnover was low, but as the older owners passed away or moved to smaller retirement dwellings, many of the homes were purchased by landlords, or younger couples who did not spend as much time on upkeep as a house demanded. In the few years they'd been there she'd witnessed a drastic change.

"What are you doing?" she asked, stopping at the edge of the street. Her body swayed as she watched Eric.

"I'm raking leaves."

"Oh. Is it fun?"

He chuckled. "No. It's just something that has to be done."

"Can I rake leaves with you?"

He stopped, leaned on the rake and glanced toward Madeline's house. Missy was sitting on the porch, her feet propped on the brick half wall with her head down in typical cell phone using position.

"Ah, no thanks. I'm almost finished."

"Ohhh!" Her voice had a whine to it, as if ready to cry.

Eric had a soft heart. He wouldn't want to make Madeline cry, but also didn't want the responsibility of watching her. That was her mother's job, even if she was incapable of doing it.

"I'm sorry. Maybe next time you can help me. Okay?"

"Okay." But it clearly wasn't okay. Her lower lip stuck out in a pout, far enough for Dina to see from the porch.

Eric went back to raking trying to finish before she cried. He worked fast perhaps hoping to finish before Madeline cried. Dina smiled and sipped her coffee only vaguely aware of the screeching tires and racing engine from down the street. The roar of a mufflerless engine drew her attention when it was half a block away. She glanced in its direction fearful the vehicle was a threat to Eric. Dina dropped the mug and launched from the chair. Her hand reaching for the gun.

Eric stopped to watch as the car flew closer. Dina reached the steps seconds before Missy screamed,

"Madeline!"

Dina glanced toward the little girl and horrified to see her stepping into the street between the two parked cars on either side of the driveway. *Oh God, no.* Eric tossed the rake aside as the entire world went into slow motion. He broke into a sprint, his powerful legs pushing to full speed in two strides. She heard him shout, "Go back, Madeline," but it came from somewhere in a hazy distance.

She tried to reach him, still afraid the car was meant for him, but he was too fast and out of reach within two of his long strides. "Eric," she called, but his focus was locked on Madeline.

Adrenaline laced fear spiked extra speed from her, but even as she missed him and understood his intent, in her heart she knew he would not arrive in time. He raised his hands and waved them above his head in a frantic attempt to catch the driver's attention. Unaware of the danger, the driver barreled forward. Dina noted he wasn't paying any attention to the street ahead. His eyes were riveted on the rear view mirror. She stopped and raised the gun thinking to fire a warning shot, but unsure of where to place it. The sound of sirens gave her pause and the reason for the driver's distraction and the speed. He was fleeing the authorities. Dina lowered the gun helpless to do anything to prevent what was about to occur.

With all his strength, Eric focused on Madeline, intent on somehow getting to her before the car slammed her into eternity. The car closed. Too fast. She knew he would not make it in time, yet still he pressed on.

"Eric," the word ripped from her soul.

Three things happened simultaneously. Madeline emerged from between the cars, the front bumper moved to within three feet of her and Eric shrieked, "Nooooo!"

Then the world went crazy.

CHAPTER

Ten

Nadina sat on the edge of the chair in the hospital room that held her son. The fact he wasn't really her son, made no difference to how she felt. Having raised him for the past fifteen years, she felt she had the right to the claim. Besides, everyone they knew in this world thought Eric was her son, and she saw no reason to dissuade their beliefs.

She rocked back and forth, elbows on knees, hands folded. She stared at the comatose boy. The doctors had been in, three of them. None had answers, but all wanted to run tests. So far they'd taken blood and had an EKG done. Eric was scheduled for an MRI next.

She didn't know what to do. Reaching him after the collision and finding him unconscious, lying in the driveway, with the little brat from across the street wailing in his arms, she was at a loss, frozen, as fear clutched her heart. The police were there in seconds, already giving pursuit to the driver. They called for an ambulance, but were confused about what occurred.

The two officers had witnessed Eric's bravery, darting in front of the onrushing car to save the girl, but were baffled about how the car made such a sudden, sharp ninety degree turn, slamming into an old oak tree, fifteen feet off the ground.

The little brat's mother ran over, suddenly all concerned about her baby. She screamed at Eric even though he was unconscious, blaming him for hurting her baby and threatening a lawsuit. Nadina clenched her fists, but held herself in check, until the young woman drew her foot back to kick Eric.

Nadina stomped her foot down on the woman's leg in mid-kick, blocking the strike. A red fire, born of fear for her son and rage at the woman, burst behind her eyes. A powerful hand shot forward clutching the woman by the throat. She yanked the frightened woman to within inches of her face. "You ever try to hurt my son again, I'll rip your throat out and your daughter will be safer for it. Now go see to her scrapes like a real mother would." She gave her a shake and shoved her backward. Between sobs, she issued legal action threats.

The officers rushed to separate them. The one holding Missy told her to clam up. "If it wasn't for that boy you were about to kick your daughter would be dead. He saved her. You owe him gratitude and then some, instead of threats. And just so you know, Officer Petry and myself will testify on his behalf. He's a hero. Now take your daughter home."

The ambulance arrived and Nadina called Nordon. He did not answer so she called the number she was instructed to memorize and never use unless it was an emergency. She judged this fit.

A man answered. "Yes."

"There's been an accident."

"What?" the tone more concerned now.

"He's hurt." She remembered she wasn't to use any names. "An ambulance has come. They're taking him to a hospital."

"You can not allow that to happen."

"But—but he needs medical attention."

"Did you call the ambulance?" the voice was angry.

"No. The police did."

"Police?" The voice rose an octave. "Did you call them?"

"No. They were already on the scene."

Silence.

"Okay. It's too late to stop it now without drawing attention. Let me know what hospital and I will deal with it. Go with them and try to stall any tests or treatments."

"Okay. I have to go. The ambulance is leaving."

"Go, but don't let him out of your sight."

The line went dead.

Upon arriving at the hospital, they were rushed into an examining room. Nadina was told to wait outside, but she stayed close enough to hear the conversation between the EMT's and the Emergency room doctor.

"I'm telling you, doc, we didn't find anything. His heart rate is low but nothing drastic. His blood pressure is slightly elevated. He was unconscious when we got there but could find no obvious cause. He has a few bumps and scrapes along his arms, consistent with diving on cement, but nothing severe. No lump or soft spot on his head. We didn't find any obvious spinal injuries, but boarded him anyway."

"Okay. Make sure the paperwork is complete," the doctor said, then he started ordering tests.

Nadina knew she should stop them somehow, but her contact wasn't there. He didn't see Eric's condition. She didn't want to disobey, but she was worried about Eric. What if he died because she refused to let them do their tests? She couldn't live with that. And since she was the only one there, she decided to say nothing.

She dug out her cell phone, an object she thought magical years earlier, but now felt as comfortable using as if she was one of these people. Dialing Nordon's number once more, this time she left a detailed message. Finished, she drew in her courage and called the secret number again.

"Yes." The same voice answered.

"We're at St. Rose's hospital."

"Did you stop the tests?"

"I wasn't allowed inside." True, but not completely.

"I'll handle it. You stay in position to protect him."

He hung up. For a moment she stared at the phone as if it were an evil entity, then, her hands began to shake. It spread to her entire body and the tears welled. She fought them, but in the end lost the struggle and she buried her head in her hands.

An hour later she was in Eric's assigned room watching, waiting and praying. Although she wondered if the Gods she prayed to could even hear her in the strange world.

CHAPTER

Eleven

Twenty minutes later, a slightly short, round man in a light gray suit, entered the room. She recognized him. His name was Samuel and he was the man they first met upon crossing over into this world. He'd gotten them set up, instructed them in how to survive in the new world and trained them how to use the strange weapons and to protect Erthyic. After pronouncing them ready, he left them to fend for themselves. At first he checked in with them a few times a year, but when he stopped coming, Dina wondered if he might be dead. She hadn't seen or heard from him in more than a decade.

He nodded at her, and moved straight for the bed. He placed a hand above Eric's head and closed his eyes. His lips moved but whatever he said, perhaps a prayer, was too low to hear. Her eyes widened as his hand began to glow, first yellow, then like a sunset, eventually turning a bright red.

She stood, awed and afraid, yet ready to move to protect her charge. What was this strange little man doing to her son? She moved forward, but even with his eyes closed he was aware of her. He held up his non-glowing hand and she stopped.

His hand drifted down Eric's body and the red glow dimmed to a soft amber, before fading out completely. Samuel's eyes fluttered open. For a moment he appeared weak and had to grab the bed to keep from falling. He bent over the bed and shook his almost bald head. His scalp reddened almost as bright as his hand. Minutes later, he straightened and turned toward her.

"Tell me what happened and what has been done here, so far."

He offered his hand and Nadina thought it was to greet her, but once his hand surrounded hers, he placed his other hand over hers and held it tight. He pulled her closer. His eyes darkened and bore deep into hers. She gasped.

"Now, speak child."

She relayed the story, but as she spoke she saw vivid images of the events playing in her mind. The vision was so real she could feel the emotions of the moment and hear the sounds from voices to backgrounds noise of birds and traffic. When her tale was finished, he held her hand a moment longer as if searching for something deeper within, perhaps details she'd forgotten or refrained from mentioning. Satisfied with what he saw or didn't see, he released the hand.

"You did well under the circumstances. Nordon is home checking the monitors to ensure this wasn't an attempt by our enemies to do damage to the rightful heir."

That thought hadn't occurred to Nadina. "You don't think they'd try to kill him, do you?"

He shrugged. "How can I know what goes through their evil minds. They really only need one of the heirs. The other is expendable. Perhaps they found the other one."

"Other one? Did his sister come through, too?"

Samuel pursed his lips as if realizing he'd said too much. He drew in a deep breath and eyed her as if coming to a decision. Then he said, "Yes, his twin sister, Elysande was saved, too."

He picked up a chart and scanned it. "Stay here and watch over him. I'll deal with the tests."

He left and Nadina sat down. Her mouth remained open since hearing Eric was not the last heir. His sister had been found and saved. She wondered why she had never been told. Maybe they saw her as a threat to their security. A weak link in their defenses. Well, they might find out how resolved she was if the threat to her son was real. She would fight to her death to keep him safe. She prayed it would never come to that, but knew the truth of her convictions deep in her soul.

***

Samuel took the elevator down and followed the signs for the lab. He found it after several turns and long hallways. He glanced through the long narrow window in the door. The room was busy. It was a third full with patients waiting to have blood work done. He spied at least half a dozen staff, perhaps more behind the doors. The lab was through a door inside the room and to the right. There'd be less people in that section, but getting to the samples he needed without being discovered would be difficult.

He entered and took a chair along the wall to the right, not eight feet from the lab door. Scanning the room, he found what he needed, then closed his eyes and called up the words to a spell. His eyes fluttered under the strain. Twenty long seconds later, someone gasped.

"Is that smoke coming from that vent?"

Voices rose, then became panicked. Someone got up and rapped on the thick translucent pane of glass on the sliding window to the receptionist. The window slid open and an unpleasant woman with a severe frown looked out.

"There's smoke coming from the ceiling," an older man said.

The woman's demeanor changed in a heartbeat. "Oh, my." She stood and pushed her large frame through the window far enough to be seen by all. "I'm not sure what it is, but to be safe, I need everyone to remain calm and evacuate the office. Please do it in an orderly fashion. Do not panic."

Everyone stood and walked toward the door. Samuel stayed seated. The waiting room cleared, but none of the staff left. *There must be another exit for them.* He waited another minute and when no one appeared, rose to try the lab door. Locked. He waved a hand over the door knob and tried again. This time the door opened.

Samuel stepped inside and closed the door behind him. The room looked and sounded deserted. He hurried toward the back and began searching for Eric's blood samples. He heard voices approaching and realized someone was coming through a side door. He stopped what he was doing, concentrated and chanted. Once again smoke curled out of the vents.

"Oh, man, I think it's spreading."

"Let's get out. The fire department's been called. They should be here in seconds."

The smoke grew thicker, now beginning to hinder Samuel. He continued his search with less concern now about leaving evidence of his presence. The door opened again.

"We've got thick smoke in here but no heat."

"Maybe a motor is going bad in one of the air conditioning units," a second voice said

"Could be, but there's no smell. Usually if something like a machine is burning out you get heat or that burning rubber smell."

It was harder for Samuel to see. He found a rack with four tubes. He picked it up and held it close to his face. The labels read, Eric Smith. Yes. He found it. He slipped the tubes from the stand, placed them in a jacket pocket and set the rack down, but in the smoke he misjudged the distance to the counter. The rack fell with a loud crack. He froze, his heart racing.

"Did you hear that?"

"Yeah, it came from back there."

"Is anyone in here? Call out. We're firemen. Will come get you."

"Hello."

Samuel had to make a hasty retreat, but he'd done such a good job on the smoke he had difficulty seeing. In fact, it was getting harder to breathe, as well. He walked with his hand extended. He coughed, the sound was like a beacon leading the firemen toward him.

His hand struck the wall and he slid his fingers along it hoping to find a door. Just as his hand brushed over the knob someone grabbed his shoulder from behind.

"I've got you. Hold on, sir. We'll get you out of

here."

Something was pressed against his mouth and he panicked.

"Relax, sir, it's just air. Breathe in. We'll have you outside in a few seconds."

Samuel allowed himself to be led. A minute later, he was standing outside with an oxygen mask on his face. The air felt good circulating through his lungs.

He drew in a deep breath and caught sight of a woman in a lab coat speaking with one of the firemen who rescued him. She turned and made right for him. He noted a security guard right behind her.

"Excuse me, sir. How did you get in the lab?"

Samuel put on a stressed and elderly voice, speaking with the mask on. "I-I don't know. When the smoke started I got confused. I was waiting to have my blood drawn. A door opened near me and I thought it was the way out. I went in and guess I was in the lab. I don't know. I was lost. Thought I was gonna die in there."

The woman eyed him suspiciously. She turned to the guard. "Stay here with him, I want to check to see if anyone exited that way. That door was locked. No way should he have been able to get inside."

She pivoted and hurried away. Samuel wasn't sure who she was going to talk to, but she had the look of a determined pit bull and not likely to let him go until she was satisfied. A check of his ID and the lack of paperwork would seal his fate. He had to get away.

He bent as if tottering and ready to fall. The guard stepped forward and wrapped a protective arm around him. Keeping him upright. Samuel muttered something the man couldn't understand. He leaned forward.

"What? Are you all right, sir? You need to sit down?"

Samuel spoke again, then placed a forefinger against the man's temple and a spark jumped. The guard's body twitched in a spasm, then collapsed into Samuel's arms. He guided him gently to the ground, placed the oxygen mask over his face and slipped away, losing himself in the crowds.

CHAPTER

Twelve

Marvin Grant turned the unmarked Ford into the main entrance of the hospital parking lot and drove around the east side. He pulled up along the curb and stopped a few yards from an animated conversation between a group of people consisting of hospital staff, firemen, and hospital security. Two CPD officers stood listening to whatever was being said, apparently by everyone at once.

Evidently a fire alarm had sounded when smoke billowed from several ducts in the lab area. No cause had been found, as yet, but the fire investigators were still working. That alone hadn't been enough to place a call for Detectives, but when a hospital administrator had detained an elderly man who had been suspiciously in the lab at the time and he'd slipped away in the confusion, security had made the call.

Grant stepped from the car and stretched his six-foot three long form. The day was warm, and the transition from air-conditioned car to outdoor heat had already caused a few beads of sweat to pop out on his forehead. He adjusted his shoulder rig, and hiked up his pants, then walked around the car to the group.

His partner, Jessie Vega, was already outside the car waiting for him. The short, barrel-chested Mexican, popped a tic tac to cover the onions from the Italian sub he hadn't had a chance to finish when the call came in. The former college wrestler still looked as though he could go head-to-head in a college match. He turned to Grant.

"Maybe we should wait until they talk themselves out."

Grant knew Vega was kidding, but he did have a point. He put hands on hips and turned his deep black face to the sun absorbing the warmth. Seconds later, he said, "Screw it. Let's make 'em shut up."

They approached the huddle. The two CPD officers looked relieved. Jackson, a black veteran patrolman who once rode with Grant, looked at his old partner and shook his head. "They called you out for this?" he asked, offering his hand.

Grant shook it and slapped his other hand on top. "Wilton, how you doing?"

"Best as . . ."

"Hear that. Yeah, security called us on a possible arson, but that sounds like a job for our trusted brothers from fire."

"My thinking, too." He nodded at Vega who did the same.

A fire captain stepped away from the now silent crowd. He stuck out his hand. "Marvin. Jessie." After shaking both men's hand, he said. "Looks like a false alarm, or at least there was no actual fire. We're still searching for the cause of the smoke, but there's been no other sightings anywhere else in the hospital. All the patients and staff were let back in about ten minutes ago."

"Good to hear," Grant said.

One of the administrators, a middle aged woman

with an angry scowl, walked toward them. Vega held up a hand and went to intercept her. "Miss, if you give us a minute to get up to speed here, we'll want to talk to you in a bit. Thanks." he gave her a gently guiding shove back toward the group and returned.

"They call you for the missing man?" Wilton asked.

"Since there's no real fire here, that'd be my guess." He turned to Dave Scalarra, the fire captain. "Unless you got something for us?"

"Nah. I can send the fire investigators report over, but we don't need you."

"Alright, Wilton, give me what you got."

"The woman over there," he flipped open a notepad and read her name, "Susan Pollard, says an elderly man was found wandering the lab during the alarm. He told her he was confused and got lost." Wilton shrugged. "Coulda happened."

Scalarra said, "A couple of our boys found him and brought him out. Gave him oxygen."

Grant nodded. Vega grunted.

Wilton continued. "She says he couldn't have gotten into the lab. She questioned her staff and no one was working with anyone resembling the man. The only place he could have been was in the waiting room and unless someone lets you in, there's no way into the lab from there."

Vega asked, "Did any of the staff go out that way during the fire?"

Wilton shook his head. "She says 'no.' All staff exited through the back door," he nodded, "right there."

"Okay," Grant said, "but then the man disappeared?"

"Yeah. She had a security guy watching him. The

guy over there getting his balls handed to him by his boss and the administrator. Guy says, the old man looked like he was going to faint. He grabbed him to keep him from falling. Next thing he remembers, he's being shaken awake by the chief of security and his wearing an oxygen mask."

Both Vega and Grant were focused with game faces on, now. Grant said, "He doesn't remember, being struck or feeling a jab from a needle."

"Nope. Nothing," Wilton said. "One second he held the guy the next he was being shaken awake."

"Huh." Grant and Vega uttered at the same time.

Wilton snorted. "You two been working together too long."

The chief of security came over, talking into a hand held radio. "Joe Perkins," he said, "Head of security. Don't know if this has anything to do with anything, but one of our patients is missing. An Eric Smith."

Grant and Vega exchanged glances. Grant put his hands on his hips. Vega crossed his arms. Their go-to poses when thinking.

"What can the possible connection be?" Grant said.

"I have no idea. Once they found out he was missing, the head nurse on that floor called the number on the admission form. No such number."

"Wait a minute," Wilton said. "Is that the kid we called in?" he turned to his partner, a rookie named Lynd. "Hey, Rook, what was the name of that kid we called the ambulance for?"

Lynd pulled a note pad from his shirt pocket and flipped through it. "Smith. Eric Smith. Why?"

"Apparently he went missing."

Susan Pollard joined them. "Is this related to my guy?"

"Don't know." All business now, Grant began giving orders. "Why don't we start at the beginning? Mr. Perkins, can you get me whatever info you can from your missing patient. It may be two separate incidents, but I want all the information before deciding that. Wilton, would you go inside and talk to anyone in the lab who might have seen the old guy. I need a description. Ms. Pollard, please tell me what you can."

CHAPTER

Thirteen

Forty-five minutes later, Vega and Grant were driving toward the address Wilton and Lynd had for the missing patient. It was different from the one the boys mother gave at the hospital. It might prove to be nothing, but it was suspicious.

"What do you think?" Vega asked.

"Not sure. It's not against the law for a patient to leave, but the false address and phone number makes it look suspicious."

"Yeah. That and what Wilton told us about the strangeness of the scene. I mean, a car fifteen feet up a tree? Come on. He had to be exaggerating."

"Yeah. Want to see that for myself."

"According to Wilton, the boy is a hero. He dove in front of a speeding car to save a little girl. Not many kids today would do that for their own mother."

"Got that right. Not from what we been seeing over the past five years."

Grant made the turn down a residential street with fifty to eighty-year-old houses, row after row, ten feet from their neighbors. Most were well maintained and cared for, but a few had run their course as livable properties and were boarded up.

"Oh man!" Vega exclaimed. "Look at that tree." he pointed.

Grant slowed and leaned forward to see through

the windshield. A good twelve to fifteen feet off the ground the large old oak bore the fresh scars of contact with something big and fast moving. A large crack ran halfway around the trunk, revealing yellowish-white wood beneath. The tree leaned toward a one-story house. It would have to be cut down before the next big wind or that house would have instant air-conditioning.

He pulled up next to the curb across from the house they had an address for. Grant let the engine idle as they observed the house. There was no one in sight, but there was an SUV in the driveway.

After a minute of observation, Grant said, "Well, let's go see what's what."

They climbed the steps to a two story, aluminum sided house and knocked on the door. No one answered. Grant tried again, this time with a little more force. The center of the door was glass so they could see a shape approach. A slim woman in her thirties pulled a curtain aside and studied them. Vega showed his badge and the woman's face went pale. She took a moment to compose herself before opening the door.

"Is this about what happened?"

"Well, yes," Grant said. "We have some questions about that and other things."

She looked from one to the other, than stepped outside and partially closed the door. "My son's sleeping, so we can talk out here."

"Is he all right?" Grant asked. "We hear he's had an eventful day."

"Yes. To say the least. He's fine. He suffered some bumps and bruises, but he'll be fine. He's just exhausted. When the fire alarms went off at the hospital, the nurse helped us down the elevator but then went back inside to assist others. Eric, my son, wanted to sleep, so I just brought him home."

"But you didn't tell anyone you were leaving?"

"Ah, no. I know that was wrong, but everyone was busy getting patients out of the hospital. I didn't want to bother anyone and frankly I also didn't want to be talked out of going home. When you knocked I was just looking up the phone number to call them. Guess I should have done that earlier." She jerked and put a hand to her chest. "That's not against the law, is it. Leaving?"

"No, but giving false information might be."

She cocked her head and knitted her brow as if confused.

"The address and phone number you gave were wrong."

"They were?" She acted surprised. "I wonder if I gave our old address. I was a bit out of it. My son was unconscious in the hospital. I wasn't thinking too well. We haven't lived here that long. I guess I got confused." She offered a smile that lacked sincerity.

"Can we look at your son to make sure he's alright?"

"Ah, he's asleep. I don't want him disturbed."

"Won't take but a minute, Mrs. Smith. I won't wake him. Just a quick peek inside his room to make sure he's okay. That's procedure," he lied, "You know, in cases where a parent takes a child from the hospital without doctor's permission or signing him out."

"Oh, ah, okay, I guess. But just one of you."

Grant nodded. She opened the door the rest of the

way and the tall detective followed her upstairs to Eric's room. She pointed and Grant cracked open the door before glancing in. He made sure the boy was breathing and didn't seem to be under any stress. Satisfied, he closed the door and went down stairs.

Back on the porch, he said, "You should call the hospital. They were in a panic when they couldn't find your son. People there could get in trouble for losing a patient."

"Oh my, I hadn't thought about that. I'll call right now."

"Okay. Good day, Mrs. Smith. You take care of that boy now. I hear he's quite the hero."

'"I will."

Grant walked down the steps and toward Vega who was examining the tree.

"What do you think?" Vega asked.

"Not sure. There's something off here. Can't say what."

"Yeah. Got the same feeling." They stared up at the tree. "What could make a car jump that high? I mean, look. It's not like there's a ramp here. How could it get that much elevation?"

"Beat's me," said Grant.

"Ah, forget it. I want to finish my sandwich."

CHAPTER

Fourteen

Fifteen Years Earlier

Phetrix prayed to the gods for the children every day since the destruction wrought by Mortas Frost. He hoped Samuel and the guardians he entrusted with their care would keep them safe. As long as Mortas had no way of finding them, they should be fine. Eventually though, they'd have to come back and reclaim the land. Until then, he'd be as careful as needed for the sake of the kingdom.

Leaving the city Mortas now controlled, Phetrix hunted for the nearest seam back to the strange world. The castle which Mortas destroyed actually housed one of the few places in Chavalon that a mage could open the seam. According to the journal Samuel left behind, there was another obscure location. It was located northwest of the village of Ulti, far to the north of where he was currently.

Remaining hidden within the forests, Phetrix remained in the shadows as much as possible. Mortas ordered Seekers to scour the land, looking for any and all who had been loyal to King Artus.

A small camp lay ahead, its fire a beacon in the waning light of day. Worried it was one of Mortas's search parties, Phetrix approached it carefully.

He crept closer, trying to stay as quiet as possible.

Weaving a spell to enhance his hearing, he listened to the group. There were four men and two women, but they weren't what he expected.

"We'll give Mortas a taste of his own medicine," one of the men said.

"Aye, Grynd, we'll make sure he pays for what he's done," one of the female voices said.

Loyalists? Mortas didn't kill them all!

With courage strengthened by the conversations he eavesdropped on, Phetrix revealed himself to the party.

"Hello! I come in peace!"

The group clambered to their weapons and held them in a defensive manner against this new intrusion.

"Who goes there?" It was the man he heard moments before, Grynd.

"Are you loyal to Mortas or the King?" one of the women asked. She had long red hair and cuts on her arms. Her tunic was torn on the side, a bloody bandage peeking through.

The two men with Grynd stepped closer, a madness in their eyes which worried Phetrix. They were both taller than Grynd. One had a bald head and the other wore short brown hair. Long beards adorned both their faces.

Judging by their garb with the white stag embroidered on their tunics, he knew their loyalties.

"I'm with the King. I'm Phetrix—"

"The mage?" the red-haired woman inquired.

"That I am. I am for the King. Does he live? Have you seen him?"

The bald man spat. "Would be nice to know, but tis

not our luck."

"You can drop your hands mage. Make a false move and Matildis will gut you." The red-haired woman smiled, spinning a knife in her hand.

"I don't doubt she will. You can be assured I am not one to cause trouble."

"What of the heirs, have you seen them?" It was the other woman. She brushed her long blonde hair to the side, revealing delicate features. Worry flashed across her face.

Phetrix shook his head. "I have not. I can only hope they were taken to safety. Mortas was determined to exterminate the royal family."

The blonde woman sighed and turned, walking to the fire by herself.

"She was a nanny for the children," Grynd said in reply to Phetrix's unvoiced question.

"This here is Gerbald," he said pointing to the bald man. It made Phetrix chuckle but the man didn't seem to see the humor in it.

"And this is Wymar. The nanny is Ancrett. We found each other in the forests after the attack and banded together. Our intent is to mount a counter to Mortas. You'd be an excellent addition to the cause, if you are who you say you are."

Phetrix waved his hands in a circular motion and created a ball of green light. He lifted his hand and it floated upwards, illuminating the camp in a murky-green glow.

"Does this answer your question?"

Matildis nodded. "Works for me. If you turn out to be sent by Mortas, no green glob of light will save you from my blade. I promise."

"Well noted."

"Now that we're all acquainted, maybe we can share our stories. I'd love to hear what you you've gone through, mage," Grynd said.

Wymar and Ancrett went to work preparing a meal for the group. The smell of roasted rabbit made Phetrix's mouth salivate. He hadn't had a decent meal since the attack.

While they were seated around the fire enjoying the meal, Gerbald started the conversation.

"How come none of us know of you, mage? We all worked in the castle for years, serving King Artus and his family. Surely we would've noticed you." Phetrix noticed several others nodding their agreement.

"The duty of mage kept me far from most servants. There were several I knew well. Nadina, Nordon, Alyanna, and others—"

"Nadina? I know her," Ancrett said. "She and I entered service about the same time."

"I knew Nordon. Big fella. He could pound down the ale!" Gerbald said.

"I saw them in the castle as the attack grew worse. I helped them escape." The group looked at Phetrix with wide eyes.

"They live? Where are they? We can grow our company larger with their help!" Grynd said.

Phetrix shrugged. "I don't know where they went. It was chaos. The last I saw, they were running from Mortas's soldiers through the halls. I can only assume they made it to safety. Hopefully, with the King and Queen."

Wymar raised a wooden mug of ale. "To the King!

Long live King Artus and Queen Griselde!"

The rest of the group joined in his toast. Phetrix relaxed. He was among like-minded people intent on making things right again. He wondered if he should tell them about the seam and the other world. Though they might fight for the king, would they understand what he did?

CHAPTER

Fifteen

Grynd kept the group loose and relaxed. Considering the circumstances, Phetrix was more than fine with it.

It had been five days since joining the group, and close to three weeks since the attack. Word had spread about a growing rebellion to the north, but that Mortas had also known about it. Whether from Seekers, those black spirit-like entities, or some other means, Phetrix didn't know. He still hadn't told the group about the seam and he was anxious to get to the farm, though the group had no intention of traveling in that direction.

Matildis stepped next to Phetrix who had been lost in thought, wondering what his next move was.

"Mage, you ever kill a man?"

Phetrix scrunched his face. "Yes I have. During the attack. I had to protect the heirs."

Matildis nodded. "Good. We might need more of that if it comes to it. Grynd got word today that a large group of loyalists have gathered in the forests around Whitemoore."

"Way up there? Does Mortas not control all of Chevalon then?"

"He does, but his hold in the north is weak. Whitemoore has sworn to him, but they look a blind eye at the loyalists. It wouldn't surprise me if it soon becomes the center of resistance to Mortas."

Phetrix stroked his long beard. Convincing the

group to join those gathered near Whitemoore might help him get to the seam faster. Each day that passed felt like another day wasted. What if Samuel didn't have the children? What if their protectors failed?

The heirs had to live at all costs. Without them, the land was cursed. The prophecy of old dictated their lives, yet Mortas destroyed that. He knew little of what he had done, but Phetrix understood the significance.

"Are we going north then?"

Matildis clapped him on his back. "We sure are! We leave in the morning."

As day broke and the camp packed up, Phetrix beamed with excitement. He packed his gear and helped the others with their own. When they were ready, Grynd led them to a nearby road heading north.

"Keep your eyes open. The road should be fine, but the Seekers are out there. All we need is one to spot us and we'd soon be in danger."

"Come on Grynd, what are you afraid of?" Gerbald chided. "We haven't been in a proper fight for weeks. My blade would like to taste blood again."

"Ever seen a Seeker? They don't have blood to spill!"

Phetrix recalled when he had seen one of those creatures, and Grynd was right. They were ephemeral beings controlled by the whims of their master. Mortas had no reservations in employing them to do his will. They were much more efficient than humans.

They passed several other travelers on the road, but none seemed to mind who they were. The group had hidden their white stag livery under tunics to help keep their identities hidden. They neared a small village and that's when Wymar spotted it.

"Up there, look!"

The group followed his hand to the sky and there it was, a Seeker. It streaked across the sky scanning the village and all roads into it.

"Don't run now, it'll spot us for sure," Phetrix said. "Just move naturally. It might not notice who we are."

They moved cautiously trying not to draw attention their way when the Seeker swooped low, right above their heads. Wymar ran.

"No!" Ancrett called out, running after him.

"Both of you stop!" Grynd cried, but it was too late.

The Seeker spun in the sky and darted for Wymar. The man foolishly tried to outrun it, but couldn't. The Seeker flew in front of him, making him fall over.

Guards from the village came running toward them. The travelers that were nearby scattered.

Ancrett helped Wymar back to his feet as the guards rushed in.

Phetrix swirled his hands, readying a spell. It would expose him to the guards but he had no choice. He had to try and save them.

Phetrix created a ball of white light and shot it forward. It streaked past Wymar and Ancrett, boring a hole through the Seeker before dissipating.

Grynd, Gerbald, and Matildis rushed toward the guards, weapons drawn and yelling.

The guards drew their swords and the three of them clashed with the three loyalists.

Gerbald swung and missed, one of the guards piercing him in his back. Matildis swung down at the guard's arm, severing it.

Wymar and Ancrett both produced weapons and joined the melee. Phetrix was unable to do much as the guards were too close to the group for him to accurately strike them with his powers. He moved around the fight, looking for ways to intervene.

Matildis was thrown to the ground, exposing one of the guards. Phetrix quickly shot a beam of fire at the man. The thin streak of flame pierced the man's chest and he fell over dead.

Wymar swung a short sword at a guard, who blocked it and countered, his blade slicing into Wymar's sword arm. He dropped his blade, clutching at the wound, when Matildis jumped in, knocking Ancrett out of the way. She parried with the guard who looked to be getting the better of her. As she tried to protect Wymar, the guard pushed the fight and nearly pierced her with his sword. Ancrett swung to the side and then lunged at the guard with her knife. She struck him in the side, the blade sinking deep into his flesh. Matildis added her own sword to the man's body and he fell over dead.

Grynd was fending off the other guard, though he seemed to be losing ground. The guard was larger and faster than him. Grynd tried to parry the strikes, but his injury made it difficult. Lines of blood ran down his injured arm, spraying on the ground.

Matildis joined Grynd. "You're no good with that arm of yours," she growled, knocking him out of the way. The guard swung his sword at her, not seeming to care who his opponent was. Grynd fell to the ground and Matildis struck at the guard, forcing him back from her injured friend.

Phetrix raced to the injured Wymar and Gerbald, hoping he could heal their wounds.

"Ancrett, hold your hand here," he commanded, placing her hand on Wymar's wound.

She did so and he channeled energy into the bloody cut. Soon, it closed enough to stop the bleeding.

"Now to Gerbald!" They took a few steps over to the other man, but as soon as Phetrix laid his hands on him, he knew it was too late.

"Aren't you going to do something?" Ancrett cried.

"I can't. Not now. It's too late."

Ancrett pounded on Gerbald's lifeless chest.

When Phetrix turned to the remaining guard, he watched helplessly as he fought with Matildis and parried her sword. He knocked her back and turned, thrusting his sword through Grynd who had been on the ground and hadn't moved quickly enough from the fight.

"No!" Phetrix cried out. Channeling his energy, he prepared to take his rage out on the guard, but Matildis had been too quick and in her rage, sliced through the guard's throat.

When the fighting ended, only Ancrett, Matildis, Wymar, and Phetrix remained. A commotion from the village stole Phetrix's attention.

"More guards. Hurry, you need to run!"

"What, we can't leave them!" Ancrett cried out.

Phetrix pointed a shaky hand at the guards coming their way. "They will kill you! Leave now!"

Matildis pulled on Ancrett. "Come on, he's right. We can fight another day."

"We'll meet again, I swear."

"We better, mage." Matildis ran into the forest with

Ancrett and the others at her side.

Phetrix wove his hands in a complex pattern then forced a stream of fire at the guards. They lunged out of the way, giving Phetrix enough time to run away.

CHAPTER

Sixteen

After the attack, Phetrix hid from prying eyes. Always with a look to the sky watching out for the Seekers, he roamed the shadows of Chevalon. Too many had died already and still he was no closer to finding the King or venturing across the seam to unite with the heirs.

Hidden within a cave in the eastern wildlands of Chevalon, he built a small fire, igniting the wet wood with his powers.

Four weeks had passed since the attack, but the memory burned within him, giving him fitful nights of sleep and anxious waking moments.

Huddled near the fire under his cloak, he desperately tried to remember the prophecy of the heirs.

According to ancient legend and secured through the centuries by the order of the Mage, heirs of the first ruler of Chevalon, King Galterius, were the rightful and anointed rulers of the land. For the most part, those rulers have been benevolent and just, ruling with peace and general harmony. There were moments of discord, such as when Prince Hemeri and Princess Ninon almost brought the kingdom to civil war, but Chevalon prospered for much of its history.

The Order of the Mage kept a secret history, a prophecy unknown to the descendants of Galterius.

Galterius's mage Edalf, known within the order as Edalf the Black, cursed the royal family. As Galterius's mage, he was a trusted advisor and confidant. At the urging of the King, Edalf produced a special blessing for the royal family, swearing that one day, royal blood would produce heirs with the ability to wield magic and when they did, they'd produce a dynasty that would last forever.

That was as much as anyone knew about Edalf outside the Order. The truth was much darker.

Edalf had fallen in love with the Queen and Galterius found out. For three days the two fought and argued with Edalf hoping to stay within the King's service, but the King, fueled by jealousy and disappointment, declared Edalf a traitor and set an execution date for him. The Queen plead with Galtarius to spare his life, and against his better judgement, agreed to banish him from the land.

Bitter and heartbroken, Edalf amended his blessing and swore that if magical heirs ever lived, they could be killed and the royal line would die with them, the land forever plunged into darkness.

His first attempt at bringing this to fruition was to pit the son and daughter of Galterius against one another. When Princess Ninon accused her brother Prince Hemeri of trying to steal her prized horse, she gathered a large following intent on crushing him. Edalf orchestrated the entire situation and the Order fought behind the scenes to restore order and reduce the damage caused by him.

Knowing what Edalf set in motion, the Order kept close to the royal family for centuries until the birth of Erthic and Elysande.

Phetrix was the first to spot their ability, the

memory clear in his mind.

"What are you doing?" he remembered asking Erthic. The boy had waved his hands, a ball of tightly woven yarn he'd been given to play with spinning in the air above him.

"Ball!" the boy replied. He was barely able to speak but Phetrix remembered the word and the floating orb vividly.

"How did you do that?"

The boy moved his hands, making the ball spin faster. He giggled and lost control, the ball falling to the floor.

Phetrix kept a close eye on him, watching for more signs, though he didn't spot any until Elysande did something similar.

The little girl was in her crib and Erthic was with her, cooing and squirming. The nanny, Alyanna, had called for the mage because of something she witnessed.

"Watch, she'll do it."

Phetrix waited, knowing the boy had been capable of wielding magic and was curious about the girl.

They watched for several minutes before Elysande moved her hands and the blanket wrapped around her slowly rose from the crib and danced. She waved her little fingers making her brother giggle at the display. When she was done, the blanket fell softly on to the mattress.

"I told you! Did you see that?"

"Alyanna, say nothing about this! Do you understand me?"

"Why not?"

"It's important none shall know. I must have your

word!"

"Fine, fine. I will say nothing."

Phetrix left and a growing knot of dread filled his belly. The prophecy had come true. If Elysande possessed the ability too, then they were in deeper trouble. Both would need protection. As long as one of them lived, he was certain the curse would not come to pass. He swore that day to never let anything happen to the children.

The fire crackled, forcing his memory to flee, returning to the present. Somehow, Mortas knew about the curse. The Order must have betrayed the King. Someone inside allowed the truth of the curse to escape their lips.

"Rhoden. Rhoden Noster." The name dripped evil. He was a rogue Mage that fled the Order and had gone silent for years. The last Phetrix had seen of him, he was at Mortas's side during the attack. It had to be him!

Phetrix stood, stretching his legs. It was no good dwelling on the past when all he could control was the present. At least for now, the children were safe with his old mentor Samuel in a land far different than their own. Hopefully they lived and hopefully Samuel could train them in the ways of magic. They'd need it to return and claim the kingdom. Until then, he'd bring the rebels together to create a force to repel Mortas.

CHAPTER

Seventeen

Phetrix climbed down from the mountains to the market in the village of Ulti where he frequently begged for food and listened attentively to the gossip of those selling and buying.

Phetrix hid among the southern mountains, living a life of solitude and contemplation. The black clad, snowflake patrols, as he had begun to call them, had concentrated their efforts to find the King and Queen to the north, making it impossible to find a way through. He didn't want to risk capture, nor did he wish to inadvertently lead Mortas' troops to the King. After the attack from the guards and the Seeker outside the village, he didn't want to get anyone else hurt. The best and safest course of action was no action at all. He found the cave and made it his home until such a time when he deemed it safe to continue his search.

For years, he waited and hoped for word that the royal family was alive, or for any sign from the other world to let him know the children were safe. The not knowing drove him to near madness in that first year, but as Mortas tightened his control on the land and more of his troops set up barracks in the town and villages, he knew his decision to hide was right.

It had been close to fifteen years since the children vanished and not a day went by that Phetrix didn't think of them or how to bring them back and reclaim the throne for the rightful heirs. Samuel would take great care of the children, as would those he thrust into their care; Nordon and Nadina for Erthic and Alyanna for Elysande. They were loyal to the King and above all else, willing to go to a far away land, to a place alien to that of their home of Chavalon.

Rain fell in cool drops and the wind blew harshly against his face. Phetrix pulled his cloak up over his bearded face to protect from the elements. Carefully, he joined the throngs of people vying for space in the market. Many arrived daily expecting deals for sale or trade and most left with neither.

Black clad guards patrolled the streets, the snowflake of Mortas emblazoned on their armor. Phetrix avoided them as much as possible. He doubted after all this time any would remember what he looked like, but why take the chance?

"Stop that boy!" one of the vendors yelled, pulling Phetrix's attention their way. A boy close to twelve years old pushed his way through the crowd carrying an apple. Two guards soon joined the chase, closing on him fast.

"Stupid people," Phetrix grumbled. Mortas had controlled all food and wares throughout Chavalon and artificially kept the prices high, forcing many families into servitude to pay off their debts. No doubt the boy was from one of those families. Almost everyone was.

Under his cloak, Phetrix waved a hand and cast a spell toward the guards, making a basket of rotting plums fall in front of them. They tripped over fruit-filled weavework and fell, slamming hard into the packed dirt ground. The boy turned back and laughed, but then slammed into another guard who had joined the pursuit from the opposite direction.

"Damn," Phetrix whispered. It was too late to save the boy without giving himself away. He had to let the guards take him. They'd probably beat him and add another five years of service onto his family, which would earn him an extra beating from his parents.

It was against this evil he hoped to one day fight. If only he could bring the children back, if they were ready to lead and if they still lived.

Hope gave him a reason to wake every day. It forced him to pray, to believe, to move forward as if Mortas would one day be overthrown.

Phetrix shook his head and made his way toward the corner he claimed for himself to beg for alms.

The rain came down harder making it difficult to see. Phetrix inched his way closer to the small store front at the corner hoping to stay as dry as possible while still able to see people walking his way.

"Alms, alms for the poor," he called out. He had a small wooden bowl he used for money laid out at his feet. At the moment it contained rain and a small coin he had placed there to seed the pot.

"Alms, alms please."

Years ago he was a master mage in the service of the king. Reduced to begging, he clung to those memories filled with hope. His abilities with magic were stronger than ever, but alone without the heirs, he had to force his desire to use them deep within himself. Unlike earlier when he tried to give the boy a chance in the market, he rarely used his abilities outside his mountain lair. Within the cave, he was safe from prying eyes. He studied and practiced his craft relentlessly, waiting for the day when he'd use it on Mortas to bring the evil man down.

To enhance his magic, he created magical talismans where he could store magic. If the time came when he needed to fight he wouldn't have to worry about depleting his energy and strength. It was a long exhausting process, but would be worth the effort when the time arose for its use. So far he had a rod, a small ruby and a ring. He never carried those items with him to the village. If a guard ever confronted him he didn't want to risk losing them. Not to mention the chance of having them stolen by any of the number of pickpockets and thieves that roamed the village. He hid the items in the cave behind protective wards only discernible by another mage.

The day passed and the rain subsided, leaving muddy streets and an empty bowl. It was getting late. Phetrix grabbed the bowl, stuffing it inside his cloak, then left the village, headed for the narrow pass leading into the mountain and his home.

As he left the village, a small pinpoint of light emerged in front of him. Resting about the height of a man and close to five horses away, it was a vibrant blue orb.

"What is this?"

Phetrix looked to either side, expecting one of Mortas' mages to appear and trap him.

The darkness around him gave him no indication who was there, if anyone.

Phetrix moved closer to the light, wonder and anxiety growing within him.

As he stood about an arms length away, the orb appeared about the size of his head. It glowed with a bluish hue and gave off a warmth. He peered closer and something moved inside.

"What sorcery is this?" He stepped closer, wary of what he might find. He swore he saw Samuel flash by within the orb, followed by images of a boy and a girl, both about the age of what Erthic and Elysande would be.

"Is this . . . could this be . . . Samuel?"

Phetrix shook with anticipation. Should he touch it? Where did it come from? Curious as to what it was, Phetrix reached out his hand and slowly inserted it into the orb. It rippled from where his hand entered, but he felt nothing other than a warmth spread over him.

Then, he pushed his face into the light.

CHAPTER

Eighteen

Inside the ball of light, strange visions bombarded Phetrix. Immediately he yanked his face out and the warmth fell from him. He breathed erratically, trying to make sense of what he'd just seen.

"This . . . this must be from Samuel."

Some of the images he saw reminded him of the time he crossed over long ago. Buildings looked similar and the wheeled chariots were like before. But the noise . . . the massive amounts of people . . . it overwhelmed him.

"This had to have been sent for a reason. I must discover its meaning."

He checked around him in the forest, wary that a trap had been set by Mortas and his wicked mage Rhoden. If he ever caught that man, he'd unleash a fury of spells on him unlike any he'd ever known. Turning his back on the Order and his mentor was a sin Phetrix wasn't ready to pardon.

The dark of night would not let him discern if anyone were nearby. The ball of light moved, scaring Phetrix.

"No! Don't leave! I've not seen yet!"

Tossing caution to the wind, he plunged his face and this time his entire body back into the warm light.

Massive buildings screamed by, the blurry motion sickening him. Overhead, blue skies dotted with white clouds were broken by objects cutting their own white lines. Below, chariots blared and people yelled. It made his heart beat faster, worried that he'd been dropped into some sort of strange battle.

The sickening motion stopped and he was left to drift lazily to the ground below.

He landed outside a large building with a red cross painted on the side with words he didn't understand. People in blue and green matching uniforms raced in and out. One of the chariots hurried past him with blue and red flashing candles on top and the same painted cross on the side. The people in green uniforms rushed to the chariot, opening the walls, and pulled out a man covered in blood laying on a moving table.

None of the people seemed to notice him. His garb was considerably different than theirs; a black, dirty robe tied around the waist with a length of rope. His scraggly beard and long stringy hair much different than the closely cropped hair and beards of the men he watched. The women wore the same uniforms. The way they attended the bloody man made him think they were some sort of mages, healing the sick and injured.

Am I at a shrine? He thought. Carefully walking, no, floating toward the moving clear doors of the shrine, he entered.

It was just as noisy inside as out. Men and women shouted at one another in words he understood. It was a different dialect than back home, but they were familiar.

Then to his left, a man he recognized ran through

the shrine and headed for two metal doors. He wore a uniform of gray and pushed something on the wall and the doors opened.

"Samuel! Samuel, it's me Phetrix!"

The man never deviated from his task. Phetrix ran to him and entered the small room as the doors closed behind him. Samuel stood next to him nervously looking up at numbers that flashed on and off.

"Samuel, it's me. Don't you recognize me?"

Samuel acted as though no one was there. Phetrix reached out to grab his shoulder but his hand went through him like a spirit.

"It's but a vision. Is this real? Has it happened already? Is it a portent of things to come?"

The room came to a halt and a ding sounded. Samuel walked right through him and entered another hall in the shrine. Phetrix ran after him, willing to see the vision through.

Samuel turned a corner, spoke to a woman seated at a desk, and followed her to a room on the far left. He nodded and the woman went back to her desk.

Samuel watched until she sat back down and then entered the room. Phetrix followed closely behind. He waved at a woman in the room to stay seated, then moved to a bed. A young man lay on the bed, eyes shut, a strange tube attached to his arm. Samuel moved straight for the bed. He placed a hand above the boy's head and closed his eyes. His lips moved but whatever he said was too low to hear. His hand began to glow, first yellow then turning a bright red.

Phetrix glanced back at the woman as Samuel placed hands on the man and mumbled words for a spell. Something about her was familiar. It hit him like a slap. It was Nadina. "Nadina," Phetrix whispered. What was she doing here?

More mature now, the young woman had grown into an attractive lady. But if seeing her now was like a slap, the sudden connection he made was a gut punch. He gasped and drifted to get a better look at the man. Then he saw him. Lying on the bed with a white sheet draped over his body.

"By the Gods! Could it be? It had to be Erthic. It must, or why would Samuel send the globe of light, or be examining the body? Body. Did the boy still live? He studied the boy, now a grown man.

Samuel spoke to Nadina. "Tell me what happened and what has been done here, so far."

The conversation lingered but Phetrix ignored it, moving closer to the man in the bed. He stepped to the right side, moving past a table with a screen similar to the one he'd seen when he first met Samuel in this strange world, but this one was black with green lines bouncing on it.

Leaning over, he realized the man was alive. Then he opened his eyes and he knew—it was Erthic! The boy lived! Hope was alive!

Then with a flash, he was ripped from the room, pulled through the shrine's walls, and back into the sky until he fell on the hard ground in the black forest.

The ball of light vanished, leaving nothing in its wake.

"No! Come back! I have so many questions!"

The sounds of the forest echoed his cries, but the vision was lost. Whoever sent it wanted him to know, the prince lived. Now, it was time to find the King and

Queen and let them know their children were alive. The end of Mortas was at hand.

CHAPTER

Nineteen

Rhoden Noster walked amongst the strange inhabitants of this amazing world as if he belonged. Dressed in a suit he'd purchased from a massive store, a department store he learned it was called, using a stolen charge card, he took in his surroundings, mentally marking certain standout landmarks, to find his way back again.

Since discovering the seam, a task he'd spent the better part of fifteen years searching for, this was his third excursion into this new world. He'd learned a lot in those previous trips. Using his magic he'd been able to gain information from some of the denizens, thus understanding the process for purchasing his local attire. He blended in with the throngs of people that wandered the streets of what he now knew as a city named Chicago.

Everywhere he looked people bustled around with no apparent purpose. Many kept their heads down averting their gaze from those around them. They stared or spoke into strange magical boxes, small enough to carry in one hand or slip into a pocket. Rhoden still hadn't fathomed their purpose, but had a feeling they had some magical property. Perhaps a form of magical protection from meeting the gaze of others on the street.

With that in mind, he set his own magical barrier to

prevent an assault. His mission was too important to be sidetracked. He stepped down a few inches onto a wider pathway and was startled by the blaring of one of the metal beasts the denizens of this world rode. He started and raised his hands to unleash a magical attack, but refrained at the last moment. As the beast sped past, the rider sent him some sort of magic in the form of hand gestures he did not recognize.

This was truly a dangerous land. Despite gathering basic information, he had much to learn and understand, but so little time. His mission came first. Rhoden vowed that when all was complete and secure, he would return to this amazing world to study it in more depth. For although danger lurked everywhere, he was intrigued and awestruck by the sheer size. The unending amount of people, the shape and size of the structures, the unimaginable products displayed and sold at the various vendors' shops as well as the strange food stuff the people shoved into their faces. Yes, this world frightened him a bit, but he was determined to understand it and eventually become its master.

Because of his plans, he had yet to inform Mortas of his discovery. He would be forced to disclose that knowledge upon producing the heirs, but until then, he kept the secret. He needed contacts here. Minions to do his bidding and teach him about surviving here.

Nothing and no one could stand in his way if he controlled the resources of this world, not even his lord and commander, Mortas Frost. At least for now. He smiled, imagining the look on the man's face when he, Rhoden dared challenge him, bringing the full might of this world down on him. Yes. It was a vision he could almost touch. But first things first. He had to find those two brat kids and return them to their own world. Which was the reason for his sojourn into this world. One of the Seekers he sent forth had spotted one of them.

Because of those previous trips, he had an inkling of what to expect. Hence, the clothes. He needed to fit in and his robes made him stand out, worse, to become a target. He feared the unknown even though he was fascinated. Until he knew more about their abilities, he didn't want to test his own skills against theirs in case their power was superior. For now he was content to walk among them and keep his head down.

He crossed the wider surface and stepped up on the opposite side. The sections of buildings soared into the sky and looked endless. He had yet to see the end of this fortress. According to the signal he received, the Seeker was still a long way off. He stopped, ducking into a recessed doorway. With a wave of his hand and a few muttered words, Rhoden connected with the creature seeing through its eyes. It had little will of its own, serving at the bidding of the one who conjured it. The almost mindless creatures did what it was instructed to do and little more. However, they were the perfect minion. Silent, nearly invisible, extremely deadly, almost impossible to kill and when given a task, continued on until success or told to cease.

This Seeker hovered over an enormous section of smaller buildings. Though similar in structure with their slanted roofs, green pastures in front and back and a metal beast sitting idly by, each had differences, their own individual look. Some were taller, some wider and in an assortment of colors, many of which Rhoden had never seen before.

The house the Seeker focused on was smaller, white and had two metal beasts next to it. Rhoden wondered if the pasture was how the creatures were fed. He sent a mental command for the Seeker to move toward the rear of the building. It did so and the sight of two people sitting on a flat surface came into view. He dared not send the Seeker lower for a better look. Although almost impossible to see at night, their translucent form did have a few observable features during the daylight, such as their black eyes, gray shaded brain and dark red heart.

The Seeker stopped directly above the two forms, he recognized as the women of this species. One was older, both wore trousers as he did, but they were short enough to be smallclothes. Their white legs were bared and the shirts they wore exposed enough skin to be scandalous back home.

He studied them for a moment, then instructed the Seeker to zero in on the younger woman. From this angle and distance Rhoden was unable to make a determination whether she was the one he sought, but nor could he rule it out. They had no description to use since they were babies when they were whisked away. They did have one telltale distinguishing feature that would make identification possible. However, those features lay hidden beneath the clothing, making a positive determination more difficult.

Something slammed into him, sending him reeling backward, and he clutched at his face. His hand came away red. He glanced up to see the offending brute only to find he had walked into a tall metal pole. Without realizing, he had started walking even though his sight was attached to the Seeker. He cursed under his breath, allowed the rage to flow into his fingers and pointed them at the pole. It began to quake and with a screeching groan of protest, bent.

Someone near him gasped. Another watcher said, "Look at that."

A third said, "Is it an earthquake?"

"No, I think that man is doing it."

With sudden realization that he was causing a scene, the very thing he wanted to avoid, Rhoden released the energy, stuck his hands in his trouser pockets, and with head down, walked swiftly away. He heard murmuring behind him, but closed his mind to the words, wanting to get as far from there as possible. It was a mistake, revealing his power to these strangers. He still had much to learn about them before allowing his true nature to be known.

Rhoden hurried on, now unsure where he was going. The link with the Seeker had been severed with the collision. He had to be more careful and must learn to keep his temper in check, at least until needed.

CHAPTER

Twenty

Rhoden walked until the larger, newer buildings gave way to older more run down and mostly abandoned structures. He noted less people and the ones he did see dressed less fancy. He likened them to the low born back home. The poor and destitute that clogged the streets with their unclean bodies and ever extended palms.

With the paths less crowded, he stopped to reconnect with the Seeker. Once the connection was reestablished, he found the younger woman had gone and one of the metal beasts was missing.

"Show me where she went," he commanded the Seeker.

It veered from the house and flew with amazing speed, over rooftops and paths. The woman was inside the beast, turning into grounds that held a long, massive building. She stopped in a row of other rides and exited. She wore strange garb. A short skirt of alternating green and white panels and a tight white top with a large green W on the front. She went through a door and was lost from view.

This was getting difficult. How could he find out if she was the lost princess if he couldn't catch up to her? He had to learn more about this world to get around it faster.

"Inform me when she leaves," he said. The Seeker

made no reply. It had limited speech, most of which was a high-pitched series of screeches when excited.

Once the connection was broken, Rhoden scanned the area searching for someone or something from which he could extract information. He walked on with little idea of what to look for or to do. Then, a tall dark man stepped from a narrow path between two run down buildings. He stood eyeing Rhoden with a curious and somewhat unnerving gaze. Rhoden felt obligated to do the same.

"I think this dude's lost," he said.

Rhoden had no idea what a dude was, but had the feeling it was him. He eyed the man with curiosity. The responding voice behind him took him by surprise. He jumped and whirled. Two more dark men stood behind him, both with wide grins. Whatever they thought was funny was not apparent to Rhoden.

The taller dark-skinned man behind him, said, "Well, maybe if he pays us we can direct him to where he wanna go."

The man in front had hair knotted in rows on his head like some sort of crop. He said, "Now, there's a good idea. It benefits everyone. We get money and he gets where he wanna be. How's that sound to you, man?"

Rhoden realized he was about to be accosted. The thought made him smile. Good. Now he would have a chance to try out his skills against someone from this world. Having already experimented on the other two trips, Rhoden knew his magic worked on this world. In fact, if anything, his magic had more power. Although, the reason why escaped him.

"What is it you want?" he asked.

All three men laughed. The one in front said, "That is an interesting question. Let me think on that a moment." He mocked thinking by putting a hand under his chin and glancing skyward. "Ah, I got it. We want your money."

"Money?" Rhoden was unfamiliar with the word, but understood the meaning. They wanted gold and silver, which he had not brought with him. But a thought came to him. He had learned a new word and might be able to learn much more by engaging the men in conversation.

" I carry no, ah, money, but I will pay you later in exchange for information."

The man in front bobbed his head once and pulled back, giving Rhoden a look of disbelief. "Information? What? We look like a public library? What kinda information you want?"

"As much as you can give. I want to understand your, ah," unsure of what to call it without giving away he was from elsewhere, he settled for, "this." He spread his arms to indicate the surroundings.

"Well, sure. Sure. We can give you all the information you want, but like I said, we needs be paid. And first."

"Like I said, I did not bring coin with me, but I will owe it to you on my next trip."

"Oh, you gonna *owe* it to us? You gonna give us your handwritten IOU?" To the men behind Rhoden he said, "Now he think we a bank or something."

The taller of the two men behind him, said, "I don't believe a man who dress in a suit don't carry no money. Let me see your wallet. No, screw that, I'll look for it myself."

He stepped forward, grabbed Rhoden's jacket and thrust a hand into the inner pocket. Anger rushed through him. His face clouded, then contorted into a mask of rage. He snapped his arm down and out of the man's grip, then shoved him backward with both hands. The startled man gave a shout as he fell back on his butt.

For a few seconds, all three men stared in amazement. Then, one by one, angry eyes swung toward him. The man in front stomped toward him, fists clenched, ready to do damage. "Oh, you asking for it now."

The upright man behind, helped his friend up. The assaulted man said, "You gonna pay for that, man." He pulled out a knife, flicked his wrist and the dulled finish of a well used but uncared for blade popped open.

This time Rhoden was prepared for their attack. His hands moved in intricate patterns. He spoke long practiced phrases and extended his hands toward the first man. An unseen force flew from his hands striking the unsuspecting man and sending him flying twenty feet in the air before crashing into a blue metal box with a curved top. The collision knocked the wind from his lungs. He dropped stunned.

Rhoden turned toward the remaining two. Both stood with jaws agape seeing their airborne friend. The man with the knife was first to recover. He lunged at Rhoden hoping to impale him, but the knife and his entire arm stopped moving as if the scene had been put on pause.

"What the . . ." the man said, as the blade turned

upward and back, moving toward him. A great strain appeared on the man's face as the blade made slow but steady progress toward his own body. He placed his other hand over the first and with every bit of strength he possessed tried to divert the blade's path, but with a sudden surge, it closed the gap and pounded into his chest. His eyes went wide, his mouth opened to emit a scream, but it seemed to catch in his throat. The third man, glanced from his friend to Rhoden, then turned and fled.

Rhoden reached out and with invisible fingers, lifted the man with the braided hair and flung him into the wall. He went limp, but Rhoden drove him into the wall once more. A sickening crack and wet smack followed and Rhoden released the body. It slid down the wall and landed in a bloody heap.

Across the path, a dark-skinned woman pointed a small rectangular shaped item at him. At first he feared it was a weapon, but when nothing happened, decided it was a personal defensive ward to protect her against Rhoden. Since she stayed on her side of the path and offered no threat against him he ignored her. She moved on, all the while keeping her ward held in front and between him and her.

The man he sent flying groaned, drawing his attention. He surveyed his handiwork with satisfaction, feeling more confident in his ability to survive and thrive in this world. Rhoden squatted in front of the still stunned man. He shook him gently, then harder when he didn't get an initial response. He moaned louder. His eyes opened in small increments, then shot open. "Nonono," he said, trying to crawl away backward. He bumped into the metal box and with nowhere to go, held his hands up in front of him like a shield. "Okay. You win. No more flying."

Rhoden was amused.

"Now then, as I said, I need information and I think you are the perfect one to give it to me."

"No problem. I'm your man. I'll tell you anything you want to know. Be happy to help." The words rushed from his mouth like water from a collapsed dam.

"Yes, I'm quite sure you'll tell me everything."

CHAPTER

Twenty-One

Rhoden had been right. The man, DeWayne, was a wealth of knowledge. So much so, he not only kept him alive, but offered to pay him for his service.

The things DeWayne told him left him dumbfounded. This world was more advanced than Chavalon. The metal creatures ridden on the hard paths were not creatures at all, but machines known as cars. Drivers controlled them and evidently, gave them the ability to move fast and go long distances in short times. After gathering as much information as his overwhelmed mind could hold, he reconnected with the Seeker and had DeWayne drive him to the location.

On the way, Rhoden studied his surroundings, taking in the structures, the people and the other vehicles on the road. He was surprised with the speed and agility of the car. "Why do you stop and sit. I need to be somewhere."

"Ah, I have to stop. It's a red light."

DeWayne gave him a funny look. "You do know what a red light is, don't ya?"

"Of course. It's that." He pointed at the traffic signal. "But why do you stop?"

"It's the law."

"Ah! The law of the land. Stop at red lights. That's annoying when you want to get someplace fast."

"Yeah. It can be. But it also keeps you from getting into wrecks with other cars. The light controls who goes and who stops."

"Who controls the lights?"

"They're automatic. You know, on timers. No one controls them. You set it, give it power and it works on its own."

"Like magic?"

"Well, yeah, I guess it is sorta like that."

He pointed at a massive building. "What is that?"

"That's a hospital?"

Rhoden had no idea what that meant.

DeWayne explained further. "It's where sick people go to get better."

"You have healers?"

"Yes, we call them doctors."

"Doctors," Rhoden repeated. "But such a large building. Do you need it that big to accommodate all of your sick?"

"Yeah, and there's three more in the area about the same size."

"Truly? You have that many sick people? Why doesn't your ruler just eliminate all the sick? The buildings could be used for some other purpose. The sick only pass it on and perform no function. Best be rid of the sick and weak."

DeWayne glanced at him with wide eyes and open mouth. "You're kidding me, right?"

"Kidding?"

"Never mind. I think I'd like living where it is you're from."

"That which I seek is in that direction."

DeWayne kept driving and Rhoden grew annoyed. "I said that way. Why didn't you turn and drive that way?"

"What, through those yards? We wouldn't get very far. A lot of them have fences. We'd never get through. Besides, someone would call the po-po. I have to stay on the streets. See, I'm turning here. At the corner."

"What is po-po?"

"The po-leese."

"Po-leese."

"You know, coming from you I think it's better you just say police. That's the law. You hear their sirens or see the blinking lights, you best get your tail running."

"Are they your ruler's army?"

"In a way, yeah. They uphold the law. You drive across someone's property and the police come and take you away."

"Make a turn here. At this street."

DeWayne followed the directions making several wrong turns because of Rhoden's lack of understanding on how to direct him.

"There," Rhoden pointed. "That is where I need to go."

DeWayne parked in a lot full of other cars.

"How many people live in this world?"

"Heck if I know," DeWayne said, "but it's in the billions."

"Billions?" Rhoden was unfamiliar with the word, but accepted that the number was great. "What is this place?"

"This is Whitford High School."

"High school?"

"Man, where you from? Don't they have schools?"

"Yes." He eyed the massive building. "I'm looking for a, ah, someone who went inside."

"Then they're either a teacher or a student. Is this person old or young?"

"Young."

"Then they a student."

"Is entering permissible?"

"Yeah, but you have to go through security and the office and tell them why you're there and who you're looking for."

That wouldn't do. "I wish to examine this school from the outside. Come."

He got out. DeWayne hesitated, but followed. They walked toward the rear of the school where a large fenced area blocked their path. The grounds held a series of fields Rhoden took for training grounds. "Explain these."

"You don't have sports where you from?"

Rhoden gave him an impatient look.

"Okay. Just asking. In front of us is a track, you know, where people run races. Over there, to the right are tennis courts. Next to that is a baseball diamond. I used to be pretty good at that and basketball. The big one to the left is the football field."

As they watched, a bell rang throughout the school. Within seconds the doors were thrown open and a wild horde of young men and women poured out. Thinking he'd been discovered and about to be assaulted, Rhoden went into a series of hand gestures ready to meet the attack head on.

CHAPTER

Twenty-Two

Grant unfolded his body from the passenger side and stepped onto the sidewalk. It had been Vega's turn to drive. They alternated daily. He didn't mind being the passenger, but Vega had a heavy foot at all times. On a call, he was a NASCAR driver, often taking chances where none were necessary. At those times, Grant often closed his eyes, praying they made it to the scene and didn't become one of their own victims to investigate.

They got a call out when the bodies of two black males were found on a city street. It had been called in by a woman who stated she'd taken a recording of the assault. He expected the men would be the latest victims in the gangland violence saga the city had been in for the last decade. It got worse every year and the powers that be were at a loss as to how to solve the problem. However, when he got there, he discovered the men had not been shot by some drive-by opposition gang. Their bodies had been beaten to death. One man had his head crushed.

He stepped under the crime scene tape and held it up for Vega. The two men surveyed the grounds. The bodies had been covered. The crime scene team was not done with them yet. Grant turned to one of the officers, a veteran named Suarez. "You first on, Daniel?"

"Yes sir. My partner and I secured the scene. Reggie's over their with the witness. Interesting viewing. Makes it pretty cut and dry, except for one thing."

Grant waited, but Suarez made him ask. "Such as . . .?"

"Oh, no. Those words are not going to come out of my mouth. You go see for yourself."

The comment piqued Grant's curiosity. He gave Suarez a sideways glance and ducked back under the tape. Suarez's partner, a rail thin black man named Reginald Pierce, was standing with a middle-aged black woman, next to a metal shopping basket. The perturbed look on her face told Grant she wanted to be anywhere but here.

"Detective Grant," Reggie said, "this is Tanya Forest. She witnessed the assault and recorded it on her cell phone."

"Hi, Ms. Forest, nice to meet you. Thank you for doing this. It will help us capture the killer of those two young men."

"If I'd a known it was gonna take this much time I'd a never called in."

"My apologies for the delay. Once I hear your statement, I'll have officer Pierce take you to the market."

"Oh, hell no! I can't be seen getting out of a cop car in this neighborhood. I'll be a marked woman. And don't be talking 'bout those two like they was saints. They was bad boys to be sure, but they didn't deserve to die. That old white man tossed them around like they's nothing. Never saw such a thing."

"Can you describe him?"

"Oh, honey, I got much better than that." She lifted

her phone and tapped a button. A video came to life--one that showed three black men accosting an older man in a suit. It looked like a typical mugging until one of the black men went flying backward, smashing into a mailbox. What made that interesting was the mugger took flight apparently without contact with the muggee. But if that was strange, the next sequence was mind-boggling. The second mugger, now wielding a knife, had the knife turned back on him. It plunged deep into his chest, but the older man never touched him. It was as if the man drove the blade into his own chest.

The third man was lifted from the ground and slammed into the wall. The second contact was responsible for the damage to the man's head. The blow that took his life.

The picture began shaking when the first man went flying. By the time the third man met his demise, the picture shook so bad it was hard to follow, but enough came through to understand the strangeness of the encounter. The woman hid at that point. She ducked behind a parked car. The picture was lost. However a minute later she got up the courage to lift the phone over the hood and continue filming. Only a portion of the scene was in view, but what could be seen, was interesting.

The older man had an extended conversation with the first victim, before walking off together. He could not see where they went, but had a face to work with. He sent the picture to his phone, then informed Ms. Forest her phone was to be held as evidence, which did not go well.

After another five minutes talking with the crime

scene techs, the two detectives left. While Vega drove, Grant watched the video several more times. It reminded him of a live magic show he'd once seen. The more he watched the fight, the more he wondered if the entire thing hadn't been staged. Well, except for the two bodies.

He shut the phone off and leaned back in the seat, eyes closed. He'd hand off the phone and hope facial recognition could put a name to the two faces. He didn't understand how the old man did what he did, but he wanted very much to meet him and ask that question.

CHAPTER

Twenty-Three

"Whoa!" DeWayne said. "Man, school's just letting out for the day. You ain't got to do that voodoo stuff. Just watch."

Rhoden did, but never released his power, ready to cast a spell that would easily take out the front row of the advancing horde, though the expenditure would take a heavy toll on his energy. Sure enough, the loud stream of evacuees, did not move toward him, but instead went to the cars. In minutes a long line of vehicles waited their turn to exit.

From a spot halfway down the building, a door was flung open and armor clad warriors burst out. Rhoden watched with curiosity. They moved toward the football field and began going through a series of warm up maneuvers, preparing for their battle training. Learning how they prepared for battle would be important knowledge.

He moved down the fence to get closer. The warriors formed a square of neat lines, then began doing organized exercises.

"Where are their weapons?"

"Weapons? Ah, if you mean their gear, it's probably stored in that shed." He pointed at a building where two green shirted men were unlocking double doors.

The door opened again and a group of women exited all wearing the same outfit he witnessed his quarry wearing. Were they warriors as well? In the princesses' case, he could understand that. Perhaps they were the ladies of court.

His heart raced as he spotted her speaking with a tall dark-skinned woman. Whatever the princess said caused the dark-woman to bark out a loud laugh. They moved on to a grassy area outside the field the warriors worked on.

Rhoden had to get closer. He had to know for sure if it was her. But how?

DeWayne leaned in close to him and whispered. "Hey, man, you got to be cool."

"Cool?"

"Yeah. You can't be staring at the girls like that or someone will think you're a perv and call the cops."

Rhoden pointed at the blonde. "I need to see her up close."

"Ah, define 'up close.' You ain't thinking some sort of sex thing, are you?"

Rhoden stared at him, confused. Then understanding dawned. "No, that is not my intent. I need to make a positive identification. But the only way to do that is to see her up close."

"It might look strange if we get closer and stare at them. What do you have to see to make this identification positive? You ain't got a picture or something?"

"No. No one has seen her in fifteen years."

"Then how . . .?"

"She has a mark on her side."

"On her side. You mean like underneath her clothes. How you gonna see that without getting her undressed? I didn't sign on for anything like that."

Rhoden continued to observe the young women as they did their own form of warm ups. Forgotten were the warriors who had now broken into smaller groups to work on skills alien in nature to him, but which revolved around an oblong ball.

After their exercise period a few of the girls walked to the fence and removed their heavy outer garments, hanging them from the fence. He slid closer. The tall dark-skinned woman blocked his view as she pulled the garment over her head. He moved away from the fence fast and was in time to see the princess raise her arms to do the same. The undershirt she wore rode up but not far enough to see what he needed.

As the outer garment cleared her head and before she lowered her arms, Rhoden cast a quick spell and with the flick of a finger sent it toward his target. The undergarment billowed as if from a strong breeze and lifted half way up her torso, exposing her midriff. He was only able to get a quick glimpse as the Princess was quick to cover herself, but what he saw caused a gasp loud enough to be heard.

The women turned to face him, all giving him the scrutiny of an outsider who did not belong.

Rhoden averted his gaze. He walked back toward DeWayne.

The taller woman said, "Was that perv eyeing us?"

The other girl, the one he now was sure was the Princess, said, "I didn't see him. What was he doing?"

"He was watching us take off our sweaters. Guess he thought he was going to see some skin."

They moved away from the fence and joined the others.

Rhoden did not look back, passing DeWayne and

heading toward the car. Once inside, he said, "I have seen what I needed. Drive."

"Okay, where to?"

"I will direct you, as I am unfamiliar with your paths."

"Roads."

"What?"

"They're roads or streets."

Rhoden nodded. Of course. He knew that. They had dirt roads back home, but he wasn't sure they were called the same thing here. He ignored the man's chatter. He had found one of the heirs. Mortas would be appeased for now, but it would not last. Once he delivered the girl, he would have to task the Seekers to find the boy. Once they were both delivered he would stay in this world, learn its ways and find a way to become its ruler. Mortas could have his world. Rhoden liked this one.

Twenty minutes later they arrived at a location a block from the seam. "I will need you to return to this spot each day. Sit and wait for my return."

"What time?"

"From morn to dark."

"That's a lot of time to be sitting here waiting for you."

"It is your task. Do not fail me. You will not like the outcome."

"Okay, sure, I'll be here. Just like you said, but didn't you say something about paying me?"

Rhoden eyed the man, then dug into a pocket. He had one coin hidden in an inner jacket pocket. He removed it and flipped the coin to him. DeWayne snatched it out of the air and studied it. "Hey, what's this?"

"A silver. Keep up your assistance and I'll reward you with gold." With that, Rhoden got out of the car and walked down the street.

"But, hey wait. This ain't real money. How am I gonna spend this?"

Rhoden continued walking.

"Dee man, what you got yourself into, now?" Dewayne said to himself. He looked at the coin and wondered if it was real silver. If so, maybe this was worth more than he thought. He knew a guy who might know a thing about coins. He looked up and to his surprise, his new boss was gone. He looked around the wide-open space, but he was nowhere to be seen. "What indeed, man?"

CHAPTER

Twenty-Four

Days after the strange vision, Phetrix beamed with excitement. He'd barely slept since then, the possibilities now endless for the future.

The sun rose in the bright blue sky and he ventured into Ulti to the corner he frequented when begging for alms. Today, his thoughts weren't on his begging or listening to pick up gossip. He was more concerned with King Artus and Queen Gresilda. He needed to find them. To let them know their children lived. But the question was, did the King and Queen still live? After all, it had been fifteen years since the fall of the kingdom. They'd been on the run for a long time.

Phetrix was confident that, if they had perished, it hadn't been at the hands of Mortas. He would have heard. Mortas would have announced to the entire kingdom of their deaths. He would have paraded their bodies through the streets of every town and village. No, Mortas had not found them.

Someone dropped a coin into his bowl. The thunk brought his attention back to the here and now.

"Alms, alms for the poor," he called out. People dressed in fine clothing dropped coins into his bowl but none bothered to look at him. Guards passed, eying him carefully as though he were a criminal. He averted their gaze, worried they might recognize him after all these years.

"Give to the needy! Please help, I have nothing."

A fellow beggar he'd known for years stumbled his way, reeking of stale ale and dung.

"Pendra, how's things?"

Phetrix acknowledged him with a nod.

"Fine, Kol. How are you?"

Kol staggered when he stepped close, his rank breath forcing Phetrix to step back. "Much better since I had me some ale. Compliments of some guard or another. I don't really care who."

Phetrix smiled. "Glad to hear it. I do hope the day is good for you."

Kol grinned, two of his bottom teeth missing. "Always when I got ale."

"Say Kol, you were one of King Artus's guards weren't you?"

Kol snapped to attention and his swimming eyes focused on Phetrix. He put his hands on Phetrix's chest and swept his gaze around them. Leaning close, he whispered, "Don't say those words out loud if you want me to live." He did another sweep, double-checking that they were alone. "Frost has ears everywhere." He made a grand flourish with his hands to emphasize his point.

"But you were in his service, were you not?"

Kol's eyes widened as he scanned the area around them again. He nodded.

"Do you know where he's hiding?"

He eyed Phetrix with suspicion and scratched at the stubble on his chin. "Dead. They're all dead. King, Queen, the children . . . those poor little children . . . all dead."

Phetrix knew it was a long shot asking this man for information, but he had to start somewhere.

"Why this sudden interest in the King's whereabouts?" Kol asked, his eyes suddenly more focused.

Phetrix hoped he hadn't made a mistake broaching the subject with this man. If he spoke of this conversation during some drunken stupor, word might get to the wrong people and he would be forced to flee. He thought that time was coming soon anyway, but he wanted it to be at his choosing and not when being pursued by guards.

"I'm getting old, Kol. Sometimes I sit here and my feeble mind wanders. I remember the old days. I recalled seeing the King riding through the countryside, ahead of a large assembly of knights. It was quite a sight. That's all. Just an old memory."

Kol nodded. Whatever control it took to keep his eyes clear had faded. "Well, old friend, best to keep those old memories up here," he tapped Phetrix's forehead, "and don't let them escape your mouth." He laughed, then belched.

"Thanks anyway. I was under the impression the King and Queen still lived. But rumors are never quite accurate, are they?"

"No, no sir they aren't." Kol hiccuped and caught himself from falling by reaching out to Phetrix.

"Pendra, you best not share thoughts like that out loud. The ears! The ears will hear and then," he made a motion across his throat with his finger as though with a knife.

"I understand. Thanks my friend. Good day to you Kol. Maybe you've had enough ale for the both of us!"

Both men laughed and Kol stumbled away, scaring

a little girl walking with her mother. Not far down the street, two guards accosted him and dragged him kicking and screaming to the magistrate where they no doubt would have him rest off his drunkenness. Eventually he'd be put into service for Mortas.

"Drunkard," he mumbled.

The day grew gray and a chilled breeze swept into the town. The amount of travelers and market-goers dwindled. Phetrix received few coins and his stomach growled. If it weren't for the Seekers, he'd use his abilities more, but it was impossible to know when they might pass. Though he hadn't seen one in a while, he knew they were still searching. Even after all these years, Mortas continued to oppress the people as he sought the heirs, decreeing constant vigilance by the Seekers.

Two years ago Mortas held a massive assembly at the building site of his new castle in the central part of Chevalon. Over three hundred men and women from all over the land attended the spectacle. Phetrix traveled to witness the ceremony as well, though in the guise of the destitute Pendra. Seekers circled the assembly above, their dark shadowy figures swirling and intertwining with one another.

Mortas stood on a wooden platform with Rhoden at his side.

"Thirteen years ago, I deposed a wicked ruler and his family. Today, we celebrate my grand new castle, the seat of your liberty!"

The invited gave a rousing cheer, but the crowd of commoners returned cautious applause.

"That despot is rumored to still be alive." Someone

in the crowd booed, a few others joining. "The time has come to end this charade. I will give any of you who find Artus and Griselde a castle and land of your own. If my Seekers find them first and you come in to claim the prize, you will be exempt from taxes for ten years if you bring them to me." A loud murmur rose amongst those gathered. Phetrix raised his eyebrows. Ten years of no taxes was a huge benefit. Mortas had claimed more money from the people than any other ruler he'd known.

"Finally, if those children are found, and brought to me alive, I will bring the captor into my family as an adopted son or daughter, with all the rights of a blood-born child."

This last decree shook the crowd and Phetrix felt a certain energy rise up. It frightened him. The rebellion had grown considerably over the years, though still in hiding. He'd had contact with a few of them over the years, choosing to remain on his own rather than live amongst them. To him, it was a safer choice.

Mortas said something to Rhoden. The evil mage lifted his head skyward, raised his hands, then spread them wide. The Seekers cried out above the assembly and they suddenly burst from their circle and sped out in all directions. The display was a message to the audience of how serious Mortas was about the capture of the royal family.

Mortas brought the attention back to himself.

"The Seekers have gone, searching for my prey. Go, beat them to it and hold me to my word!"

Mortas raised his hands and Phetrix gasped. His hands . . . glowed. Though faint, he caught the sight. Did Rhoden do that? Or . . . did Mortas now posses the ability to wield magic?

He quickly left the assembly, worried that the fight was going to be more dire than he imagined.

Now, as he marched his way through Ulti, he periodically checked the sky for the dark shadows. He hadn't seen any this day, but they were always there. Somewhere.

CHAPTER

Twenty-Five

Several weeks passed and Phetrix carefully questioned the other beggars in Ulti. As undesirables under Mortas's reign, he reasoned they had little to gain from turning him in. Even if they did, they'd face a severe punishment from Mortas for being homeless beggars interfering with his loyal subjects. They were often transient and never stayed in one town for too long.

No one seemed to know anything about the King or Queen. At least if they did, they weren't sharing the information. Maybe they thought he was a spy and would turn them in? He tried hard to convince them otherwise, but still . . . it could be holding them back.

Hope was fading and he grew desperate. It had been a long time since he'd met with anyone from the rebellion. He worried that maybe they no longer believed they could win. If they'd lost that hope, then Mortas truly did win, no matter if Samuel kept the heirs alive or not. He wouldn't believe it. He couldn't give in to despair. Artus and Griselde were alive, somewhere. They had to be.

Phetrix tried a different tactic. He listened for clues from passersby, hoping he'd hear something that would give him a glimmer of truth that he'd follow to the end.

If they were alive, they were never spoken of. Most likely he'd have to find someone to pay for information so he saved everything given to him, resorting to stealing food when hungry, hoping the guards never caught him.

When he figured he had enough coins saved, he went into the village tavern—the Winking Bear—and cautiously waited for some drunk guard or traveler with a loose tongue.

The first night he went, he discovered nothing. The tavern was subdued more than usual and very little information was to be found. The only bit he did discover was that Mortas had directed his Seekers to the west as rumors of the heirs had spread. It was impossible since they were with Samuel in the other world, but at least it directed Mortas away from the truth.

For the next several nights, nothing of importance bubbled to the surface of the conversations he had with strangers. He pried, he bought more ale, but nothing was shared.

About a week after he started, he was running out of coins and patience. It was a weak plan, but he hoped for more than what he got.

He bought a mug of ale and watched the crowd inside, looking for anyone who might help him with what he wanted. Across the room, a man he didn't recognize sat against the wall with a large brimmed black hat pulled low over his eyes. Several people approached him through the evening and Phetrix watched more than one drop a few coins on the table for him. Hoping that he might have information to help, Phetrix approached the man.

Before he could say anything, he felt a tug on his

arm. He turned and Kol smiled at him.

"Pendra, come over here. It's been awhile."

Annoyed at his interruption, Phetrix reluctantly agreed. He watched as more people approached the man who barely spoke a word to them, but nodded as they dropped coins on the table. He'd grown quite a large pile already.

"Kol, I was about to talk to that man. What is it that's so important?"

"Keep your voice down. You don't want to go anywhere near him. He works for Frost. He'll slit your throat before you get your question out."

"But how did you—"

"Listen to me." Kol grabbed Phetrix's cloak and yanked him close. With Kol's lips touching his ear, he whispered, "The King—?"

Phetrix opened his eyes wide. "Yes?"

"He lives."

The words rang louder than any bell or explosion he'd ever heard. The destruction of the castle on the night of the attack was nothing compared to those two words. *He lives.*

Phetrix grabbed him by the shoulders and shook him. "Are you sure? How can this be? How do you know?"

"Be quiet! If anyone hears this, we're both dead men!"

Something nagged at Phetrix and a cold descended over him. He searched deep into Kol's eyes. "I thought you were taken by the guards."

Kol ran a hand through his hair and looked down, speaking quietly. "I was. I paid the price."

"What price was that, old friend? Did it happen to

involve selling me out?"

A look of shock, then fear ran through Kol's eyes. "No. No, never. I would never give those bastards anyone. No, I paid," he lifted his tunic, "with blood." Several ragged, red puckered scars lined his chest. "They held me down and had their fun carving on me like I was a roasted wild boar. Believe me, I wouldn't give them anyone. Once they were done with me they took me out back and dumped me in a pigsty." He lowered the shirt. "You have nothing to fear from me, Pendra. My hate for them is far too strong to ever take their coin to sell someone out."

Phetrix was shocked at the sight, but did not allow the scars to satisfy his query. Instead, he bore deep into the man's eyes, and found no sign of falsehood. He relaxed.

"But how do you know about—" He wanted to say the words but they were not in a place to speak freely. What did Kol know that he didn't weeks ago? How did he come to this conclusion?

"Come with me. It's not safe in here." Kol turned and walked out the door with Phetrix at his heels.

As they passed the table where Mortas' man sat collecting coins, Phetrix thought he detected a slight alteration in the tilt of the man's head, as if his eyes followed their exit. The thought tightened a band across his chest. The angst did not release him easy. There was something sinister about the man. Phetrix was determined to stay as far away from the man as he could.

CHAPTER

Twenty-Six

Phetrix nervously walked next to Kol as the man led him to a dark alley behind the tavern. Guards were no where to be found and Kol waited as a few drunks stumbled out of the tavern. Once they were out of earshot, he began.

"You asked about the King?"

Phetrix nodded.

"When I was locked up, there was another prisoner with me. He sat in a pool of his own vomit and reeked of ale and tobacco. Not that I was much better."

A man walked by the alley and Kol waited, his eyes darting back and forth looking for trouble.

"After several days of sobering up, he and I got to talking. Nearly two months ago, he'd been in the forest west of Ulti living off the land when he stumbled across a small camp. Hungry, he snuck in at night and stole bread and ale. As he was leaving, he tripped on a log he hadn't seen in the dark and fell into one of the tents. Inside the tent was an older man who was built like a boulder. Well, it didn't take long for the older man to beat up my new friend. Bloodied his lip and gave him a swollen eye he did."

"What's this have to do with King Artus? Is there a point to your rambling?" Phetrix leaned close but didn't smell ale on Kol. He'd cleaned up quite a bit since his imprisonment.

Kol glared at him, then continued.

"The man alerted the rest of the camp and soon my friend was surrounded by three other men and a woman. They questioned him, worried he was a spy sent from Mortas. As they were about to kill him, one of the men—at the urging of the woman—put a halt to the proceedings. He declared, 'Spare this man. Let him be. He's done nothing we wouldn't do in his situation. It's clear he's not allied against us. Mortas has not sent him.'"

"Are you implying that was the King? That's not enough evidence to convince me!"

Kol brushed off the insult and started again.

"The woman there came to the man's side. 'Artus, you are wise in letting him go. He poses no threat. The more we can show mercy to, the better we will be when the time comes. Mortas would never be as gracious as you.'"

Kol fell silent, letting the speech sink in.

"So you're telling me you believe the King is alive based on the testimony of a fellow drunk who you happened to be in a cell with?"

"That's exactly what I'm telling you. Why would he lie to me? What's to gain? We were both locked up and awaiting judgment. You asked me a while back if I heard anything and I hadn't. I've stayed far away from those rebels to the north. But since we last spoke . . ." he trailed off, looking down. His hand moved across his chest. "We need to restore the rightful heirs. The reign of Mortas has done much harm to our people." When he looked back up, his eyes glistened.

"Kol, what happened to you? Who were you before

you became like me, a poor man trying to live off the mercy provided by others?"

Kol rubbed his hands together and thought about the question before answering.

"At one time, I was a young squire in the King's service tending to horses and the stables. After a few years I rose to the level of King's Guard. I was so proud to wear his colors. To be considered one of the elite." The gleam in his eyes faded, his gaze drifted down. "Now look at me. I'm nothing. A homeless beggar. A no-one who guards feel free to carve up without recriminations."

When he looked up, tears filled his eyes. "I was there, Pendra. Fifteen years ago, I was there. Do you know what it was like to see all those people murdered because of Mortas's ego? He had no claim to the throne but his evil knew no bounds. Amongst the slaughter many of my fellow guard fled. I called them cowards and urged them to stand and fight to the last man. But none listened. I found myself alone. As the enemy streamed into the castle, I took a look around me and knew in my heart all was lost. Then, to my never-ending shame, I . . . I ran from the destruction and certain death, too. I was weak and knew no better than the others who ran. What makes it worse is I never saw what happened to the royal family. My fear and desire for my own self-preservation won out over my pledge to protect the King and his family at all costs."

He wiped the tears away with a violent swipe of his arm. His voice found steel. "Don't you see. I was a failure. A coward. But no more. If the King still lives, he shall have my sword again and this time I will not fail in my duty."

Phetrix inhaled deep. There was much to Kol he didn't know and this revelation was stunning.

"You were at the castle when the attack came? Do you know what happened to the children?"

"Erthic and Elysande? No. I've always hoped they made it out alive, but I never found out their fate."

Phetrix wondered how much he'd be able to trust Kol. Did their mutual bond of poverty give them enough to go on?

"What was it about this story this friend of yours told you that makes you believe him?"

"The way he described the man and woman sounded exactly like King Artus and Queen Gresilda. I could picture them in my mind, older of course."

"I'm still not convinced."

Kol's face flashed anger. "I didn't come here to argue with you! Again, when you asked me about the King before, I had nothing. I've since discovered what I believe to be a fact and my first thought was to share it with you. I've been looking for you ever since I got out yesterday. Believe me or not, I don't care. I've done what I came here for. I hope the information is useful. If not, then I've wasted my time. It doesn't matter. I intend on finding the King. I'm leaving this village and going west into the forest. If I die searching for King Artus, then at least I died doing something. I'm done with begging because the reign of Mortas has forced me to it!"

Kol stormed off, muttering something about heirs and life. Phetrix considered running after him to tell him his story, but then backed off. If Kol was right and this tale told in a dungeon was true, then it was best he soon figured out how to contact Samuel. It had been years since he attempted to enter the other realm, fearing he'd lead Mortas to the heirs and all hope be lost. Maybe now it was time to bring them back and reclaim the kingdom.

CHAPTER

Twenty-Seven

Four men in suits stepped out from nowhere onto the road. A sharp blast of a horn startled them and a car veered away. Three of the men were ready for battle, but Rhoden lifted a hand to restrain them.

The car bounced over a curb and stopped, the irate driver got out screaming and shaking a threatening hand. He was large both in height and girth. He advanced on them and Mortas eyed him with curiosity.

As the man drew closer, Mortas nodded to one of his large companions. The man moved to intercept. Seeing him approach, the driver halted. The coloring of his face altered to a brighter red. He sputtered something, pivoted and hurried back to his car. Once inside, he sped away.

"What strange world is this?" Mortas said.

Rhoden smiled. "As they say here, you ain't seen nothing yet. But, let me remind you, we need to keep to ourselves. That means as little interaction with the locals as possible. Let me do the talking."

Rhoden had returned two days in a row spending time with DeWayne, learning the local customs, terms and items. He was far from expert, but had a better understanding of the people and the geography. On the second trip he gave DeWayne a list of items they would need including, purchasing clothing for the men. They guessed at the sizes and Dwayne placed the orders after taking several gold coins to an exchange shop. The value of the coins was near six thousand dollars, however the owner paid a mere two thousand and that after a lot of haggling. After paying for everything Rhoden required, he still had a few hundred dollars left, not counting the two gold coins he'd kept for himself.

Rhoden appeared the next day, collected the clothes and disappeared back into his world. An hour later the four men entered the new world.

As prearranged, DeWayne arrived driving a van. Rhoden opened the passenger door and climbed in while Mortas and his two henchmen eyed the vehicle with uncertainty, before getting inside.

"Do you have the information I requested?"

"Yeah. She's at the school right now getting ready for the football game."

"Take us there."

"You got it, boss."

DeWayne drove and Rhoden watched the other men's reactions. Even Mortas's eyes widened as the car accelerated. He remained amazed as the surroundings passed by. But though his curiosity might have been stimulated, he made no comment.

"These machines are the horses of this world," Rhoden explained.

Mortas did not reply, but took in the details. After serving Mortas for many years, Rhoden recognized the man's looks. The one he saw now, was the smug 'I can conquer this land,' look. That bothered Rhoden. He needed to get a foothold in this new land before Mortas had the opportunity to invade it himself. If Rhoden could find both heirs they would keep Mortas occupied for a while, giving Rhoden the chance to make his move. His main advantage was that Mortas had no idea how to create the seam. Though he'd taken to practising magic over the past few years, his skill was low and his patience for the preciseness of the art was lacking. He tended toward the more powerful destruction spells rather than ones requiring finesse.

They parked in the crowded school lot and walked toward the football stadium. DeWayne paid for five tickets and they entered. Rhoden scanned the grounds for what he now understood were cheerleaders and this was a football game, a contest of strength and speed and shear brute force. From the little he'd seen so far, he thought he'd enjoy watching this football.

He spied the princess and climbed into the bleachers directly in front of her. They sat and watched for a while, before Mortas said, "Why have you brought me here?"

"The girl on the field in front of us. The blonde with her hair pulled back into what they call a ponytail, is the princess."

Mortas narrowed his gaze and leaned forward. He studied her for a moment. "How can you be sure?"

He held a hand out and DeWayne placed binoculars in the palm. He lifted them to his eyes and focused them on the girl. Once adjusted he handed them to Mortas.

"She bears the mark."

Mortas placed the glasses against his eyes and jumped in his seat. His hand extended as if trying to touch the image in front of his eyes. His fingers brushed the hat off the head of the man sitting in front. The man spun angrily.

"Hey. You looking for trouble?"

Mortas gave an evil smile. "I'm always looking for trouble."

"Oh yeah? Well, you found it, buddy."

He stood, fists clenched, ready to fight. The two men Mortas brought with him stood as well. The man on the right growled. The offended man froze seeing that both men were bigger than him.

DeWayne said, "They're not from here. It was an accident. He didn't mean anything by it."

The man looked down at Mortas, who flashed a wicked smile. He looked from the twin towers and said, "Well, okay then. As long as it wasn't done on purpose." He turned around, picked up his hat and moved several rows down.

The teams took the field and the cheerleaders broke into a chant. They bounced up and down, kicked and leaped. After the kickoff, as the cheers died, the princess set her fluffy flower like things down and reached up to adjust whatever held up her hair. The shirt with the big W on the front rode up exposing her firm flat stomach. However, it did not show enough to see the identifying mark.

As he had done on the first day, Rhoden cast a spell and the heavy shirt lifted high enough to cover her face, exposing much more than intended. On her left side was a light brown, semi-circular shape, about six inches wide.

Trying to get a closer look, Mortas leaned forward. He gasped and stared harder through the glasses.

"Have you seen the mark up close?"

"No sir, only from a distance, but I'm almost positive it's the mark—the half crown."

"We need to get up close to be certain."

A roar went up from the fans as the home team ran to the far end of the field. Rhoden didn't understand the game, but loved the full contact action.

Mortas stood. "We'll take her now."

Rhoden grabbed his master's arm and held tight. The man fumed at the touch. Fire flamed in his eyes.

"My Lord, this is a different world than ours. We cannot just march down and take her. The people here will react and stop you. It is better to take her when no one else is around."

"These peons cannot stand before my power."

"Possibly so, but look how many you'd have to take out before you got free. Is it worth the risk of failure? We don't know enough of their capabilities. Look at how many might descend upon us."

Mortas scanned the crowd. "What do you suggest?"

"I still have the Seeker overhead watching her. We follow her home and take her there, where fewer people will raise a hand to protect her."

Mortas looked at the princess once more. "That will work."

"Hey, buddy, you want to sit down so the rest of us can see."

Mortas shot the man a withering glare. A second man and a woman added their voices to the complaint.

DeWayne nudged Rhoden. "We should leave before this gets ugly."

"What does one's ugliness have to do with this?"

"Cause there's all kinds of ugly and one is when a crowd turns on you in such a way as to beat you ugly."

Rhoden looked at the angry faces around him. "We should go make preparations, my Lord."

Mortas took one more look at the princess, nodded and handed the glasses to Rhoden. He passed them to DeWayne. The four men walked down the bleachers leaving DeWayne to follow.

CHAPTER
Twenty-Eight

They reached the van as another loud cheer rose from the stands.

"Where to, boss?" DeWayne said.

"Drive, I'll direct you," Rhoden said.

Rhoden connected with the Seeker and followed it to the neighborhood where he'd first discovered the princess. He instructed DeWayne to park several houses down from the target property. Lights were on inside the home.

"We should get inside before she comes home," Rhoden said. "We can take her in private then move her to the van."

DeWayne parked. Rhoden turned to face Mortas. "Sire, I'll take one of the men and secure the house. Once that's done we'll wait for her arrival. The driver can pull the van up and we can transfer her."

Mortas eyes narrowed. Rhoden spoke in a hurry to avoid the confrontation he knew was coming. "Sire, I'm trying to protect you. Although I am more familiar than you about this strange world, I still do not know what to expect. I have no idea of their capabilities. I would prefer to handle this first to keep you from danger."

Mortas gave an almost imperceptible nod. Rhoden turned to DeWayne. "When you see her arrive, move the car forward. Be ready to leave as soon as we're inside."

"Yes sir."

Rhoden exited and one of the bodyguards followed. As they reached the house, the lights went out. He froze afraid they had been sighted. The house next door had a line of bushes at the front corner of its property. Rhoden ducked behind them to observe the house. Nothing happened for several minutes, but something about the scene looked wrong, though he could not put his finger on what. Without a word to the bodyguard, he crossed to the side of the house, then to the fenced yard behind. He scaled the fence and heard the bodyguard as his bulk made the fence squeal.

Rhoden was about to step toward the rear door, when the hairs on the back of his neck rose. His skin tingled with alarm. He called up a basic discovery spell and swept his right arm in an arc over his head, sending the energy outward. A fine green hue formed in horizontal lines along the house.

He shook off the momentary surprise, understanding now what had made him on edge. There were others in this world capable of magic. Or was this the work of one man? Of course Phetrix would set up protection for the young royals. Well, the old magician was no match for his skills.

Rhoden strode to the middle of the yard, scanned the entire width of the structure and spoke words in a language long dead, calling forth energies only few knew existed. Though this world's sources were weaker than at home, he was still able to draw what he needed.

Swinging his arms in opposing circles, joining the wrists at the completion of the move, he gave the words volume, then yanked his arms apart. Though unseen to the normal eye, the wards protecting the house were ripped open, leaving a large gap surrounding the glass doors.

Satisfied with his work, Rhoden stepped forward and tried the door. Locked. Opening a lock was child's play compared to dispelling a ward. But the effort it took to pass the wards took their toll. Rhoden was forced to rest a moment before opening the door. Not that it took much energy, but if he faced more magic inside, he wanted to be able to respond with power. He spoke the words, and reached for the handle. A spark lit, burning his fingers and repelling him backward.

Shocked and confused, he studied the structure while cradling his injured fingers, wondering what he had missed. With another wave of his arms he sent out another discovery spell, only to find the wards had re-established their position around the house.

The sight angered him. Phetrix was not in the same class of mage as he. His spells did not have the power nor complexity to stand before him. The thought was unthinkable. Once more he dispelled the wards and once more was repelled at the door. Whoever set these wards had superior knowledge and ability. Perhaps this world had mages of its own.

Shaking his hand, he once more found the wards had regenerated. This was impossible. He refused to accept Phetrix was his superior in anything.

"I'm going to cut the wards off. As soon as I do, you need to get inside the house by whatever means necessary. Understood?"

The big man nodded.

Rhoden prepared his spell and cleared his mind. This would take more effort than he predicted and may leave him drained. He made the gestures, but when it came time to pull his arms apart to cast the wards aside, this time, he held his arms wide to keep them apart. He strained from the effort. His muscles protested as if he were holding a heavy weight. The bodyguard picked up a chair and pitched it through the glass doors.

He then stepped through as Rhoden released his grip. Once an opening was made the wards would only cover to that point. He started forward as a violent explosion came from within the house and the bodyguard flew backward out of the building.

Rhoden paused staring open-mouthed at the bloody heap off mangled flesh at his feet.

"They told me you'd come."

The voice startled Rhoden almost as much as the explosion. He looked up to see a woman standing in the doorway brandishing what he assumed was a local weapon of some sort. Wisps of smoke curled up from the twin cylinders, their dark openings aimed at him. Without knowing what the weapon did, Rhoden dove to the side as another explosion occurred. A stinging pain ignited in his leg.

He rolled, coming to one knee. The weapon was bent in half, the woman worked with frantic movements jamming small cylinders inside the chambers. He had no idea what they did, but did not wish to find out. Unsure he had adequate power left to cast a spell strong enough to stop her from hurling the fiery bolts at him, he switched to the stored power in his ring, aimed it at her and spoke the word that released the energy. Two vivid red streams raced outward, catching the woman as if in a net and hurtled her back inside the house.

Rhoden raced forward, leaped over the blood-soaked mutilated body, across the threshold and went inside the dwelling. He slid a knife out from within his jacket. The house was dark, but something moaned and writhed to his left. He snapped his fingers and a small globe of light formed in his palm. He lifted his hand and pushed it forward, revealing the woman pinned against the wall, held in place by the red strands.

Her wild eyes went wider as he approached her. She struggled in vain, kicking her legs, but the harder she fought the tighter the bands became. She gasped for breath and ceased moving. She eyed him with mixed hate and fear.

"So, you are the guardian of the princess."

Before he could say another word, a light shown from outside the house. He stepped to the front window and spied a vehicle on the path next to the house. A sinister smile spread across his face as the princess got out.

"Too bad you failed in your duty."

CHAPTER

Twenty-Nine

The door rattled as a key was inserted. The woman tried to cry out, but Rhoden silenced her with a backhand swipe, sending another red stream that slapped across her mouth. Her head bounced hard as the band stuck her to the wall, serving the dual purpose of knocking her out.

Rhoden stepped back into the shadows of the darkened house. The door opened and excited voices talked over each other. The princess entered, followed by a tall slender dark-skinned girl. The same one he had seen her with before.

"I know, right?" the second girl said. "He's so big and girl, those muscles."

The princess laughed, then froze, steps from the door. "Why are the lights off?" she asked.

"Was there a power outage?" the second girl said.

"Maybe. Mom. Are you here?" She reached for the light switch and flicked it on. It took a moment for her eyes to adjust, but the sight of her mother stuck to the wall two feet off the floor left the terrified girl speechless.

The other girl said, "What the ..."

A man stood in the door frame. In an instant he understood the danger and moved to enter. Rhoden swept his arm out and the door slammed shut behind the girls. They jumped and screamed. The man pounded on the door further exciting the girls into near hysteria.

Rhoden stepped forward. He grabbed the princess by the arm and pulled her roughly behind him.

"Wait. Who ...? Help! Shree."

Shree ran forward, grabbed Rhoden's fingers and ripped them back with such force one cracked. He howled in pain, his grip broken. The two girls ran for the door, as it burst open, slamming against the wall. The man stepped in, fire in his eyes and fury in his massive fists. He eyed the stranger in his house and without looking at the girls yelled, "Run!"

He advanced on Rhoden. Still fighting the pain and with his finger bent backward, casting a defensive spell would be difficult. He reached into a pocket with the uninjured hand and pulled out the amulet he usually wore around his neck, but before he could activate the power stored within, the man was upon him.

A fist struck with blinding speed, shattering his jaw and sending him sprawling. He tumbled in a heap beneath the woman's feet. The amulet flew across the room. The man paused, shocked at the sight of his wife hanging on the wall, her head lolled to the side, like some grotesque piece of modern art. Then the shock morphed to rage and he advanced with murder in his eyes.

Rhoden was too stunned to react. He attempted to crawl away from the crazed man, but he had nowhere to run. His hands extended for him and he whimpered in defense. But just as he feared the end had come, a savage blow was dealt to the man, driving him to his knees.

Behind him stood the second bodyguard, a man equal in size and ability. But, as he moved to deliver the killing blow, the guardian shot a foot back, connecting with the bodyguard's knee, driving it backward. The bodyguard let out a shrill shriek and dropped hard to the floor.

The guardian stood, shook his head once and kicked the guard so hard in the face it lifted him off the floor and slammed him down on his back. He paused over the man to ensure he wasn't getting back up, then returned his attention to Rhoden.

Rhoden crawled into a corner, curled his knees to his chest and cried out in despair. He wanted to close his eyes, to not witness what was about to be done to him, but they refused to obey. His panicked mind raced for a spell he could use without the use of his fingers, but none came to mind. In desperation, he lifted the hand with the broken finger and the ring. The guardian stormed forward, glancing once at his mate hanging from the wall and lifted his mammoth boot to stomp the life out of Rhoden. However, before the foot descended, a blinding white bolt of light, sharp as a physical sword, pierced him from behind. The tip protruded from his massive chest. He arced backward, his face contorted in a mask of agony. He emitted no sound other than a faint gurgling deep within his barrel chest, then the magical blade vanished and the guardian fell to the floor with a heavy thud, revealing Mortas, an evil sneer on his dark face and a glow of triumph in his eyes.

For a moment there was only silence, then, from the outer door, screams filled the house. The two girls stood on the porch, their hands bound by something unseen. Their faces contorted in horror at the fallen guardian. DeWayne stood behind them, his mouth agape, his face ashen.

"Come Rhoden," Mortas said, in a voice so deep and different from his own.

Rhoden wondered what demon Mortas made a deal with to wield such raw and powerful magic. Or perhaps he *was* possessed by some demon. One thing was sure. Rhoden had underestimated his king's power.

Mortas said, "Let us be away from this place."

Rhoden regrouped his runaway emotions and bottled his fear. He had never been hit so hard before. His jaw hurt, his finger ached and his body was drained. Standing, he clutched the injured hand and walked to the door. DeWayne was already pushing the girls toward the street. Mortas bent over his bodyguard, whispered a few words and snapped his fingers. The man's eyes shot open. He stood in a stiff manner as if someone else controlled his strings.

They reached the van and a strange new sound filled the night.

DeWayne said, "Someone called the cops, man. We gotsta go." Rhoden climbed in the front. The bodyguard sat in the back with the two captive girls, but Mortas, with a fire still lit in his eyes, stood waiting to see what would arrive.

"Sir," DeWayne said to Rhoden, panic replacing nervous. "He don't want to be messing with the police."

Rhoden leaned out the window. "Your highness, we have what we came for. Let us be gone."

Mortas blinked twice as if coming out of a trance.

Without a word, he entered the van and DeWayne sped off, the sliding door still open and Mortas' head hanging out to see what was coming. Sirens growing in volume, the reflection of the police lights bouncing off houses on the next block, DeWayne made a sharp, angled turn at high speed, that rocked everyone back in their seats.

The girls screamed at the top of their lungs until Mortas grew annoyed. He looked at the zombie-like guard and mumbled something while he snapped his finger. The guard wrapped an arm around each girls' head and clamped a massive hand over their mouths.

Mortas faced the girls and waved his hands. He spoke several words and their eyes glazed over. The guard lowered his arms and sat back. They now had the same zombie expression on their face.

Rhoden pushed aside his pain and reflected on what he'd learned tonight about his king. The man had obviously been practicing dark magic. Creating a zombie took the skill of a higher-level mage. If Mortas could do that, he'd progressed much farther than Rhoden thought. What else could Mortas do? And what did the discovery of this new ability mean for him.

As the car raced toward their escape route, Rhoden wondered if he'd let slip his plans somehow. Clearly, the king had been developing his magic without Rhoden's assistance, or even discussing it with him. The thought gave Rhoden more than one bad feeling. He'd have to tread easy for the next few days and try to decipher what it all meant.

CHAPTER

Thirty

Phetrix struggled with the knowledge Kol shared. Was it real? Did it matter where he gained it? He desperately wanted it to be true, but now he had a choice to make.

Would he chase after a rumor and seek the King and Queen or would he return to the seam and the other dimension to rejoin Samuel and bring the heirs back?

The choice was maddening. As he blindly walked along the hard packed dirt streets, he barely registered the commotion happening several blocks away. It wasn't until a wiry man slammed into him, knocking him over, that he realized what was going on.

"Sorry mister!"

The man, dirty with his ribs showing through a tear in his shirt, scrambled to his feet and ran away.

"Get back here you filthy rebel!"

Two guards dressed in black with the white snowflake emblazoned on their chests chased the man. Overhead, a Seeker flew across the sky.

Phetrix grumbled. The man might well have been a rebel, but he doubted if the man knew anything about the King and Queen. Their cause had attracted a great many people, mostly those who were crushed under the weight of Mortas's reign.

The guards followed the man around a corner. The

Seeker screeched above and darted downward.

"Poor soul. Be free my friend."

Phetrix hoped the man wasn't caught, but felt the outcome was a foregone conclusion.

Returning to his thoughts, he wondered what to do with Kol's information.

He'd spent his life with the knowledge of the prophecy. When he discovered Erthic's ability, it was stunning. Never had he imagined he'd be the one to shepherd the chosen ones to maturity. Elysande's ability sealed their fate. He knew then they were in grave danger. Not that he knew an attack was imminent, but there had always been an undercurrent of discontent in the kingdom, it manifesting in the attack lead by Mortas.

"Whenever there is more than one person gathered together, there is always a chance of people getting angry," Samuel was fond of saying. It was his way of soothing Phetrix's fears that an uprising was imminent. As it turned out, it was, but with Mortas leading the way, it took on a more sinister tone.

"Mortas Frost," Phetrix mumbled. He'd made his way through Ulti and was on a lonely road which led to the mountains and his home within their slopes.

Mortas was an angry man and had always been for as long as Phetrix remembered. Serving within his army felt like the right thing until the evil side of Mortas reared up. When he looked back on his time with him, it was a wonder he hadn't seen the darkness earlier.

Phetrix risked drawing attention to himself and created a small ball of flame to light his way. He'd grown tired of traveling in darkness. Loneliness was a constant companion he wanted to be rid of.

The road wound through the forest, the darkness of night oppressive. Eventually, the road narrowed until it fell away to the foot of the mountains. Only those familiar with the path would notice it. Phetrix had used his powers to cover them as best he could without losing the path himself.

An owl sounded in the distance. Twigs snapped, making him spin toward the sound. *Did the Seekers spot me?*

Forcing the ball of flame to grow larger, he saw the source of his fear. A small raccoon scurried across the forest floor, chittering at his bright light.

Phetrix clutched his chest, letting the deep breath out he didn't realize he was holding in.

"I need to make things right. It's far past time I fixed what Mortas destroyed. The heirs are ready. They'll have to be. The rebels will need guidance, and I can do that."

He turned from the raccoon and found his way back home.

Inside the cave, he covered the entrance with a bearskin and ignited a torch. In the far back corner he'd hidden the journal Samuel left for him. Inside were spells and information regarding the other world. Phetrix dug out the book and sat next to the torch to read.

The rebels need guidance. They need hope. They need the heirs. If I could find the King and Queen, maybe I'd be able to find the other seam and take us all through it. With Samuel waiting, we'd have the power to overcome anything.

Phetrix opened the book, but the vision of the man

running from the guards returned to his memory. He had to do something now to make things right. He had to act with an urgency he'd lacked for years. What good would the heirs be if there were no people to lead?

Tossing the book against the wall, Phetrix pushed his face into his hands. He'd had the ability to stop all this, if only he would've tried. With the powers he possessed, he should have been able to do more than whisk away the children with a few caregivers he forced into service.

Did he do the right thing? Had he miscalculated the lengths by which Mortas intended on securing his reign? Thinking of the rebel running from the guards, clinging to the hope that one day the nightmare would all be over, made him angry. Mostly at himself. He was better than that. He'd need to be to set things right.

CHAPTER

Thirty-One

The day after Kol's admission, Phetrix awoke with a pounding headache. A thunderstorm erupted outside the cave, the thunder doing nothing to help his head. Rubbing his temples, he wove a spell of healing on himself that dulled the pain. Had another mage done the same to him, it would've rid him entirely of the throbbing.

However, it had been close to five years since he met with anyone from the Order. As far as he knew they were all dead, executed by Mortas.

Mortas decreed they be disbanded and labeled as traitors, with Rhoden the lone exception. Phetrix was in Ulti the day he heard the news, begging for alms and attentively listening to the crowd.

At first he heard it in passing.

"Did you hear Mortas has outlawed the Order?" one woman said to another as they walked by, ignoring the haggard looking old man Phetrix portrayed himself to be.

"But they've protected Chevalon since as long as anyone can remember," the woman replied.

"I know, but they've gone afoul of his ways."

Their conversation followed them, their words piquing his interest.

Another couple walked by, dropped a coin in his bowl, and were discussing the current situation.

"Can you believe it? He actually did it," the woman said to the man.

"He's gone mad with his own power. It's amazing what—"

Phetrix lost the rest of their words as others walked by, a concerned murmur rising amongst them.

He never thought it possible that the Order would be subject to the whims of a ruler. They were above petty political differences. That is, until Mortas disrupted the entire world order.

Even during the near civil war caused by Prince Hemeri and Princess Ninon, the Order remained neutral. They were above the fray and they were responsible for rebuilding what those two tried to destroy.

To hear rumors of its demise was disheartening.

Phetrix picked up his bowl and left his corner, seeking to validate the claims he'd heard.

Near the town center, a large group of people gathered as a crier sent by Mortas repeated his decrees.

"By the order of Mortas Frost, rightful ruler and sovereign of Chevalon . . ."

The crowd groaned at the words, forcing a grin on Phetrix's face.

"The Order of Mages, commonly referred to as The Order, is hereby banished and outlawed from the land. Furthermore, any who dare assist or openly aid the Order will face immediate punishment up to and including execution by hanging. The Order is an enemy of the Crown, and our benevolent leader Mortas Frost shall rid the scourge from Chevalon."

Phetrix pushed his chin back in place, his mouth

opening wider as the man spoke.

"How could this be?" someone in the crowd said.

"What about Rhoden?" another countered.

An unease he'd never seen before rippled through the crowd.

"Mortas has lost his mind!" a man yelled, forcing the crier to stop repeating himself. Three guards rushed into the mass of people and dragged him away. The crowd grew silent and worried, their feelings evident in their scared faces as they watched the man pulled across the dirt street.

Clearing his throat, the crier began again. "By the order of Mortas Frost, rightful ruler..."

Phetrix shook his head and walked away, unwilling to concede the fact that Mortas crossed a line none had ever dared to cross. The Order was always there. It had protected Kings, Queens, and the common people since its inception. How could one man disrupt it all?

The reign of Mortas grew more worrisome by the day and the need to repair the damage done more necessary.

When he left the town center, he passed an old woman who winked at him. *Odd*, he thought, but continued on. At the next corner, she was there again, this time waving him toward her. He ignored the old lady and turned the corner, heading for the road out of the town.

When he got a block away, she was there again.

"Who are you?" he asked. "Why do you follow me?"

She approached him slowly, then her eyes flashed a bright blue.

"What?" he mumbled.

"Phetrix, come with me."

She turned abruptly and walked to a nearby house where she entered, leaving the door open. Hearing his name spoken aloud almost made him jump out of his skin. No one knew who he was, he was certain of it. Whoever she was, he had to find out what she wanted. Grasping a small amount of magic to protect himself, he followed her inside.

The door slammed shut behind him and a torch ignited to life.

"What's going on here?"

"Relax mage, you're safe here." The woman turned to him and her wrinkled face smoothed out, revealing a younger version of the woman. Her hair turned from white to dark brown.

"Who . . . who are you?"

"Mathilda, from the Order. Have you heard the blasphemy of Mortas?"

He slowly nodded, unsure what to think of the current situation.

"The Order has gone in hiding. You will do well to follow suit. You've been in the mountains, right? Good. Remain there as long as possible until we can sort this whole thing out."

"What 'we' are you referring to? Who are you Mathilda?"

"I serve the Grand Mage, Samuel. I hear you know his whereabouts?"

Phetrix gasped. He never realized Samuel would have more contacts back in this world. It made sense and he should have seen it sooner.

"I do. I met him once."

"Then you know the heirs are safe."

He nodded. At least he hoped they were safe.

"Our situation here is dire. The need for the King to return is greater than ever."

"Is he alive?"

"We . . . we've yet to find him. We have turned our hope to the heirs. Only they can repel the evil wrought by Mortas. We can help them."

"By sticking our heads in the ground and doing nothing?"

Mathilda stepped closer, her bright blue eyes piercing him. "By staying alive until the day comes."

When Phetrix finally left that meeting, his mind found it difficult to wrap itself around the current situation. The Order was aware of the heirs. They were now outlawed by Mortas. They wanted to stay hidden for what . . . a time in the future?

Thinking back on it now, it made his head throb harder. Though Mathilda was the last of the Order he'd met, he sure could use her power to rid him of the pain rattling inside his head.

The thunder boomed again outside and he closed his eyes, trying to will away the memories.

CHAPTER

Thirty-Two

Phetrix went into Ulti, preparing to take his street corner and beg for alms as he'd done for some time now, when he noticed guards harassing a couple. Initially he walked past, not wanting to engage them, but the further away he got, the more guilt crept in and forced him into action.

It had been a couple days since he met Mathilda, but he learned a couple valuable things from her. The first was that the Order remained alive, in one form or another. They were hiding in plain sight. Who knows how many he'd seen over the years? They were actively trying to find the King and knew about what he did with the heirs. No doubt Samuel played a major role in all of that.

The second thing he learned was how to disguise himself. Mathilda's magic fooled even him, and he should've known better. When they were talking, he studied the remnants of the spell and dissected them until he could cast it himself. Feeling he had a good grasp of it, he ran behind the nearest building into a deserted alley and cast the spell on himself, turning him into a younger man without a beard.

Once he felt sure it worked, he stepped into the street to confront the guards. More to test his magic than anything else, though helping the couple just made sense.

"What are you two doing to these people? What did they do wrong?"

One of the guards turned to him. "Leave us be! This is none of your concern!"

The woman looked at him with terror in her eyes. Her companion wasn't a large man and he seemed overwhelmed by the guards.

"I asked you two idiots a question. What crime could they possibly have committed that you fools felt the need to bother them?"

"Fools? Your tongue is gonna get you in trouble!" the other guard said. He was taller with a scar across his face.

"I won't tolerate your ignorance. Why are you messing with them?"

The guards tossed the couple to the hard dirt road and turned to him.

The shorter guard cracked his knuckles. "Ignorance? Mortas will not be pleased that we have people questioning his servants."

"I don't really care. What I do care about is why you find the need to bully these people. As far as I can tell, they've done nothing wrong."

He felt a surge of adrenaline course through him. It had been a long time since he found himself in a physical altercation. He didn't intend on this turning into one either, but the possibility made him ready just in case.

"That's our decision to make," the tall guard said. "Now you get to come with us!"

The guards moved quickly toward him, but Phetrix waved his hand and caught them in an invisible grip.

"What the--" the tall one said, "We've got a mage! Outlaw! You belong on the gallows!"

Phetrix waved his hand and stuffed both their mouths with air so they couldn't speak.

Turning to either side, he used his power to push the guards out of the street and into the alley. He turned to the couple.

"I suggest you two leave. The rebellion is alive. The heirs are returning. Quickly now, go! Spread the news. The heirs are coming!"

The pair picked each other off the ground and stared at him with wide eyes.

"The heirs?" the man asked. His question made Phetrix pause. Everyone knew them, didn't they?

"The children of King Artus and Queen Griselde? They live! They will restore this land to its former glory. Mortas will be vanquished."

The guards struggled against his magical grip, but Phetrix held firm. Fortunately no one else had come near them.

The woman seemed to understand him. "The heirs. Erthic and Elysande. They're alive? That means—" She slapped her partner's arm. "They live!" Hope flashed across her face.

"No go before more guards arrive! I'll take care of these two, but you have to go. I can take care of myself. Hurry. Spread the word. The heirs shall return!"

The couple nodded and ran off. Phetrix turned his attention to the guards.

"As for you two, I think you need to learn a lesson."

As he was about to let loose all his frustrations, he felt the concealment spell waver. *Oh no*, he thought. If his disguise vanished, he'd have no way of returning to the town later without being noticed. He had two choices.

He could dispose of the guards, killing them so they'd never be able to reveal his true self, or he could flee. He considered killing them the better option but before he could weave the spell to do so, a family walked by the alley and stopped, noticing how the guards were in a state of frozen movement. They had a young girl with them that pointed at Phetrix.

"Mage?" she asked in a sweet voice.

Her father glared at him, then yelled loudly. "We have someone from the Order! Guards! We have a traitor!"

Phetrix cursed to himself. He was there to help them! Mortas would never be the ruler they needed! He was a monster and must be stopped, why can't they see that?

He ran from the alley while the father raced after him, shouting and calling attention his way. Phetrix spun, cast a spell to trip him up, and ran away. The man fell to the ground and rolled to a stop. Guards ran after him, but he turned through narrow alleys and winding streets, eventually losing his disguise. He slowed his pace and stooped like an older man. Rounding a building, he took up position on the corner like he normally would and nervously waited as the guards ran past him.

He breathed a sigh of relief when they didn't recognize him and scoured the streets searching for the younger man he no longer was. It had been an interesting experiment, but he cursed himself for going too far. He should have known better. After fifteen years, many had given up on the return of the King and Queen. There were also those too young to remember a time without Mortas as the ruler and still others who had been under his rule for so long, the King was no longer relevant. A large portion of the population held King Artus to blame for their current situation. They felt abandoned, left to the mercy of Mortas and his minions.

As Phetrix settled into his begging position, he wondered if there would be enough support for the King to return. If the support had been there years ago, why hadn't he made the attempt already? Maybe the real reason was the people no longer stood behind him and accepted him as their rightful ruler.

All I wanted to do was help. Have we become so jaded that Mortas seems like the right choice for us? The rebels have been in hiding too long. The Order has lost its luster. Something has to be done. The heirs must come back to make things right.

Alone, he couldn't force the change Chevalon needed. With others, he'd be able to bring back the glory of the kingdom. He only hoped it wasn't too late.

CHAPTER

Thirty-Three

Three days after he attacked the guards, Phetrix returned to Ulti and the street corner he frequented. The day was warm and not a cloud drifted in the sky. It was almost enough for him to forget the dire situation the kingdom was in.

Then he heard the crier.

"Mortas is coming! Mortas is coming! Gather in the town square. Mortas is coming!"

People ran past him, jostling with one another to get as close to Ulti's central square as they could. Children cried as their parents dragged them through the throng of people. Mothers scolded their little ones, fathers laid swats to their bottoms.

Phetrix watched, anxiety growing as the crowd grew. *Why would he be here today?*

Ulti was a small town never gaining the eye of any ruler as far as he remembered, which is why he chose the place. It was far enough from the capital to avoid detection and other than the market, it wasn't of significance.

A shadow raced across the ground and Phetrix looked up. Five Seekers streaked across the sky, their black wispy forms a stain against the azure sky.

Oh no, are they here for me?

The thought of his actions against the guards causing all this worried him. Mortas was unpredictable and ruthless. If what Phetrix did brought his ire ...

He packed up his bowl and joined the throng of people, pushing his way closer in order to hear what was to come.

The crier continued his calls. "Mortas is coming! Mortas is coming! Gather in the town square. Mortas is coming!"

Moments later, the Seekers swirled above the crowd, silencing them. Phetrix felt a nervous calm growing within the assembled people. They were just as worried as he was.

The guards sliced through the crowd to open a path. People cursed and shouted back at the guards who pushed them out of the way. Phetrix focused on the opening the guards held. It took several minutes before anyone appeared.

Then he saw him.

Mortas.

Clad in black armor, the white snowflake blazing bright on his chest, the sigil of House Frost. They were an old family from the far north. They claimed ancestry to the same lineage as King Artus though the connection was never substantiated. The Order kept identical records as those that were housed in the castle before Mortas destroyed it. Phetrix spent many days studying the unbroken line that connected to Artus and then the children. House Frost was never part of it. They weren't even married into the family as far as he could tell.

Mortas smiled and waved as he marched through the crowd. His massive black stallion, had the same arrogant air as its rider, it's sheen so glossy as to appear oiled. The people were quiet, a low rumbling reverberating amongst them as shock registered on their faces. Mortas stopped in the center of the crowd and coaxed his beast into a complete circle so he could view the crowd from his superior position

A cart was pulled in place by two horses and Mortas dismounted on to it. Once there, he raised his hands high and the anxious murmuring within the crowd ceased.

"My lovely subjects, it is my honor to visit your beautiful village." He paused and tepid applause greeted him. He continued, unphased by the response.

The smile faded for an instant, then he recovered. "Very well then. Let me get straight to the matter at hand."

"The King lives!" someone cried out. Phetrix whipped his head in the man's direction and watched as guards rushed at him and dragged him from the assembly. He screamed as they pulled him away. "The King lives! Mortas is a fraud! The heirs will return!"

The poor man. They'll kill him for sure, Phetrix thought.

Mortas grinned as they hauled the screaming man away.

"My subjects," he cried out, stealing their attention away from the man, "It has come to my attention that one of you is from the Order. One of you is a traitorous mage." A murmur rose amongst the assembly, people turning to their neighbors unsure what to think or do.

"I have decreed the Order to be a subversive organization that shall not be tolerated within my lands. You have heard the law spoken to you plainly. Because of this act, I have come here to snuff out this traitor and restore proper order to your town and my kingdom. If you do not produce this deceiver to me and my guards within a week, I will have no recourse but to garrison this town with my followers and enact martial law. I will not tolerate disobedience. I will not allow such sedition to go unchecked."

He paused, the words sinking in the crowd.

Phetrix felt ill. This calamity was his fault. His rash actions brought this punishment to innocent people.

"We'll find the mage," a woman cried out. Several others agreed, but not as many as Phetrix assumed would. Maybe they were ready for the heirs to return? Maybe they understood the evil Mortas to be.

Soon, others echoed the woman and swore to flush out the mage, making Phetrix's earlier optimism drop with each added voice.

Mortas raised his hand, quieting the crowd.

"I expect to find this traitor with your help. We cannot let this mage run amongst you freely. Whoever it is, they are dangerous and seek to pit you against me. They must be stopped."

He climbed down from the cart and followed his escort through the crowd.

Phetrix shook his head. How could the people buy his logic? Mortas was evil, how could they not see it?

As he left the assembly, Phetrix overheard several people talk amongst themselves.

"I'd never turn in a mage to that fool Mortas. He's done more harm than any ruler I've ever know," one man said. His companion, an older man agreed.

"The Order has always been looking out for us. I

trust they're doing the same now."

A woman on the other side of Phetrix spoke to her children in a quiet voice. "You see a mage, you tell me. Don't share it with the guards. You hear me? They are good and honorable people protecting us from harm."

"Yes mother," the two girls replied.

Phetrix left the assembly with a renewed spirit. Whatever Mortas had done to try and crush his opposition was creating a different effect. If Phetrix could finally bring the heirs back, he'd have support for their cause. Time was running short. Action needed to be taken.

CHAPTER

Thirty-Four

Two weeks after Kol revealed his information, Phetrix decided to attempt crossing through the seam. It had been years since he had tried and there were few places left within Chavalon where he could perform the feat. The old burned ruins of the castle were no longer feasible, but a farm outside the city proper housed a location he could enter.

When he studied the book Samuel had him read, there were five locations within Chavalon where the older mage documented seams that led to alternate worlds. It was a three days journey from where he lived. Packing his belongings in a tattered leather bag, he slung it on his shoulder and left.

Seekers were a constant threat. Rhoden and Mortas forced the creatures to stay on constant vigilance. Until Mortas's appearance, he hadn't seen one in months, but he also stayed far away from most clusters of people as he lived within the wild mountains.

If he knew where the seams were, maybe Rhoden did as well. The wily mage wasn't as proficient as he with his powers, often resorting to storing energy within objects to assist him when he needed it. Phetrix had no need of such tricks. His power and knowledge were so great, he had all he needed. However, as late, he too had been storing magic, especially as he learned new spells he wasn't as used to casting on a more regular or practical basis.

Setting off at daybreak, Phetrix hiked down the mountain and entered the forest to the west of Ulti. He worked his way through thick brush and forest overgrown with thistle and vines. It was an unforgiving place, but afforded him the protection he desired from prying eyes of stray Seekers.

"Can Kol be trusted? Are his sources true?"

Phetrix spoke aloud, giving himself company along the desolate journey.

Could the drunkard be trusted? Was the King still alive? Maybe he ought to find him first instead of driving headlong into the tear and possibly giving away the location of the heirs.

After fifteen years of hiding, he wanted something different. "I must find them. Samuel sent me a message. I must heed it. What will come of Chevalon if I ignore his call?"

Birds chirped and rabbits scurried across dried leaves. The afternoon sun was hidden behind a canopy of bright green and Phetrix moved with a purpose through the forest.

He didn't fully trust Kol, but something about his conviction made him at least question it. If he was wrong, what did he lose? Living in the mountain cave brought him no closer to reconciliation with the King. If he did something, maybe he'd have a chance to approach the growing rebellion with the heirs.

"What am I doing? Running like a fool to try something that will probably kill me or get someone killed. Pah!"

A nearby squirrel chattered at him when he yelled

out.

Ignoring the pest, Phetrix pushed his way through to a small stream where he rested and sipped the cool water.

Scanning the sky above for Seekers and the sun, Phetrix decided to stay where he was for the night. He got about as far as he expected and with nightfall, he dared not press his luck.

When the morning's crisp air awakened him, he set off again on his trek to the farm and the seam with which to travel to the strange world.

"How are we going to rid Chevalon of Mortas? What are we going to do once we bring the heirs back? Will they be ready?"

He hoped so. The entire reason they were whisked away was for their safety and training. As young as they were when Mortas attacked, they didn't stand a chance to defeat him. They were too young to realize the potential of their power. Hopefully over the years, Samuel would have them ready. Somehow.

Near midday of the second day, Phetrix stumbled upon a body.

"What is this?"

Cautiously, he approached the bloated and decaying body. It appeared to be a man much younger than himself. The man had been huge. Though animals and insects had been devouring it, the frame stretched well over six feet.

Phetrix scanned the area and noticed a charred circle nearby and when he looked at the entire area, he realized it was once a camp. Grass and leaves smashed in patterns showed where cots lay and people walked.

"They must have been here for some time. What

were they doing out here?"

Holding his nose, he bent closer to the man hoping to discover what caused his death. There were no obvious signs of struggle or trauma other than a single hole in the center of his forehead. At first he thought it was from an arrow, but it was a perfectly round hole and appeared to have been singed on the inside as though from a bolt of fire.

"Rhoden? Mortas? There are few with this kind of power."

Phetrix moved the man's leather coat to the side and gasped.

"The story . . . it is true!"

The man wore a shirt of linen emblazoned with the sign of King Artus—the white stag.

"Impossible," he whispered. The symbol had been wiped from Chevalon by Mortas in the years following his overthrow. This man must have been part of the rebellion, but this far south?

"What if the King was here?"

It couldn't be true, and he knew it the moment he spoke it aloud.

"So who are you? What did this to you and where are the rest of your people?"

A chill went up his spine as he considered his discovery.

Then, a crash in the forest to his right startled him. He crouched, waiting for the intruder. Holding on to his powers, ready to strike at the unwanted visitor, Phetrix leaned closer to the dead, stinking body, trying to use it for cover when a man appeared. Laughing at himself, Phetrix rose.

"Kol? What are you doing here?"

CHAPTER

Thirty-Five

Kol embraced Phetrix, turning away from the dead body.

"I told you Pendra, my friend's story was true. Look at the evidence!"

"But why are you here? How did you find me?"

"Actually, I wasn't looking for you. I was trying to find the King to pledge my services to him once again, but all I found was this man. And you!"

Phetrix took a few steps away, pondering his next move. Should he tell him who he really was? How far did he trust Kol? Could he possibly be serving Mortas?

"Kol, tell me the truth. Tell me why you're here." Phetrix waved his hand, using a spell he hadn't tried in a long time. If successful, Kol had no choice but to tell the truth.

"I've already said. I'm here to pledge myself to the King." Kol's eyes glassed over as the spell took hold.

"What tavern did we meet in a few days ago?"

Kol cocked his head to the side. "The Winking Bear. Why?"

"Who is Mortas to you?"

"The no good bastard is an evil usurper, killing the royals for pleasure. He wants ultimate power for the price of royal blood. He's not my lord."

Phetrix turned, thought about what he'd do next, when Kol interrupted him.

"Pendra, would you join me? Come with me and we'll find the King. He lives, I know it!"

"Phetrix."

"What?"

"My name is Phetrix."

Kol's face scrunched. "I've heard that name. Everyone has. You can't truly be him. He was a wise—"

Phetrix raised his hand and produced a ball of light that hovered between them.

"Mage? You could say that."

"But how did you escape? The castle burned!"

"I'm not easily killed."

"But the children! Do you know what happened to them?"

Phetrix nodded. "They are safe, for now. At least, I believe them to be."

"Why hide this from me? We've been asking for alms together for a long time now. Why did you never share this before? Why would one of the most powerful mages of all Chevalon be reduced to beggary?"

Phetrix raised a hand to stop the questions.

"I'm in hiding much like yourself. Sympathizers to King Artus are not highly regarded these days. I prefer to keep my head on my shoulders."

"But you have great power! You could easily stop any attack!"

"I'm not invincible nor am I powerful enough to take on an entire army devoted to Mortas."

"But . . ."

Phetrix waved his hand and the light vanished. "I know where the heirs are."

Kol's eyes widened. "You do? Where?"

"Safe."

"Can we bring them to the King? If the rebellion knew they were alive, things might change quickly."

"Since when did you become such a noble supporter?"

Kol hung his head. "I've spent far too long with ale. I've tried to drown my past and run as far away from it as possible. When I was in that cell, something happened to me. Hearing that maybe the King still lived sparked a hope within me I hadn't known for years. Living as we have is meaningless. Living with hope, well that drives a man to do many wonderful things."

"Aye that it does. And that brings us to this place with this man, dead and stinking before us. He bears the white stag. If he wasn't with the King, then he was at least an ally."

Kol walked around the dead man, inspecting him carefully.

"All I see is a hole in his head. What do you think did such a thing?"

"I can conjure a spell producing tendrils of flame capable of doing such a thing. My guess is someone else has that ability as well."

"Rhoden?"

Phetrix nodded. "He's also ruthless enough to murder a man with his powers. I estimate he's been dead about three days. The growth around him and the rot taking over his flesh are no older than that."

"Where's the rest then? If a camp was here, where'd everyone else go?"

"Kol my friend, that is the mystery of the moment. Now, do we try and figure that out or do we seek the heirs and bring them back?"

Kol thought about the question carefully then answered. "The heirs. If the King has hidden this long without detection, he can do so a bit longer. If the heirs can be brought back, we will ignite a rebellion far more powerful than whatever it was that did that to the poor man," he said pointing at the dead body.

Phetrix smiled. "That's what I was thinking as well. Shall we go then?"

"After we bury him. We should respect our dead."

"That we shall. We can take care of our friend here and then we'll be off. Where we're going, you'll be amazed."

They spent over an hour digging a shallow grave with two thick branches they found and gently laid the dead man within. They covered him and said a quick prayer.

"Are you ready Kol?"

"As ready as can be expected. So tell me about where we're going."

"Words will never do it justice. When you see what I've seen, you'll understand."

They left the grave behind and together marched toward the north, toward the farm where Phetrix could open the seam and enter into a world far different than their own. Hopefully when they got there, the heirs would be ready. The vision Samuel sent him seemed to indicate something happened, but what?

CHAPTER

Thirty-Six

Phetrix and Kol moved carefully through the forest, their gaze constantly going to the sky, wary of Seekers revealing their movement. Kol kept up with Phetrix's pace, and soon they rested for the night, waiting till the morning to travel again. Once the sun rose, they were off, moving closer to the farm and the unknown beyond.

"Kol, how well did you know that person in the dungeon with you?"

"Not well. He and I had been there before, but that's about it. Why?"

"I wonder why you felt compelled to believe him? What was it about his story that made you think, 'Yeah, I can trust him.'"

"The detail of his story seemed too real. We both saw the result of it. He told the truth. That man we left yesterday is proof!"

"It's proof that the rebellion exists, and close to us. What if your friend was a spy? What if he was sent by Mortas to secure more important captives? I still don't buy the entire story, but I have hope the King lives. If not, we must unite the rebels to the heirs and reclaim this land. Mortas has done great destruction to it all."

"He has, huh?" The strange voice made both men spin in the direction from where it came. Two men in black armor with the snowflake of Mortas emblazoned on it were nearby, their swords at the ready.

"Who might you men be?" Phetrix asked.

"We do the asking, not you." The man was large with a stomach to match. His long hair was straight and greasy and scars ran along his face, indicating he'd seen many fights in the past. The other man was thinner, older, and had a gray beard that almost touched the tip of the snowflake. Both looked tired and weary.

"My name is Pendra and this is my companion Harold. We travel in peace, seeking food and shelter."

"Food? Are you daring to defy Mortas by growing your own without his consent? You know the penalty for that, don't you?"

Kol puffed out his chest. "Mortas cannot rule like this! He's not the rightful heir to the throne and his ways are evil. They bring a plague upon the land."

What was Kol doing?

"A rebel, eh? You ready to die for those remarks?"

The thinner man stepped closer. "You might not want to provoke my friend here. His temper is about as short as he is."

Kol stepped even closer. "The heirs will conquer this land and Mortas will be dead."

Oh dear Gods, what has he done?

"An interesting statement from a drunkard. A dark man stepped from behind a large tree. He wore a black brimmed hat and a heavy black cape, but had no emblem on his chest.

Phetrix felt Kol stiffen beside him. A quick glance showed Kol's color had drained. The sight was enough to pale his own face. The new arrival stepped closer. He oozed confidence. The sinister sneer suggested he was going to enjoy whatever was about to befall them.

Closer, Phetrix recognized him as the man from the tavern collecting money, though for what purpose, he still did not know why. Kol's words came back to him. *You don't want him. He works for Mortas. He'd cut your throat before you got your question out.*

The dark-complexioned man rested one hand on his sword and the other one on his belt. "I've been watching the two of you. I think you're up to no good. In fact, I'd go as far as to say you're conspiring to overthrow the King. A traitorous notion that will result in your deaths."

Phetrix tried to avoid a conflict, though he knew it was already too late. "Please, we don't want trouble. As this gentleman stated, my friend is a drunkard. He knows not what he's saying. We're just two beggars on our way to a new town."

Kol objected. "I am not drunk. I haven't had a drink in weeks. And I don't regret my words. You are the real traitors. You overthrew the rightful king."

The man laughed. "What you're forgetting drunkard, is that your king has been gone for fifteen years. Mortas rules now."

"Well, maybe not for long. Isn't that right, Phetrix?"

"Phetrix?" the dark man said. Suddenly he didn't appear to be so sure of himself. He slipped back allowing the two guards to have clearance. If the guards recognized the name they showed no sign.

Phetrix watched the reaction from the dark man and knew he had been outed. He had to stop him. If word got out that he was alive, and in the area, no one would be safe.

The heavier guard rushed toward Kol. Despite his bold words Kol was unprepared for an attack, his rusted sword still hanging from the rope he used for a belt.

"Treason like that deserves death," the guard said, raising his sword for what he surely believed to be an easy kill. "Do you have any last words?"

"I do. Goodbye," Phetrix said. The mage swirled his hands through the air creating a ball of wind and released it at the guards. The powerful blast knocked them both off their feet.

"He's a rebel! One of the wicked spell wielders!" the thin guard cried out. The two guards regained their footing and held their swords out, poised to strike.

Phetrix looked past them searching for the dark man, but he was gone, vanished like a spirit. He turned his attention to the two guards. they stood ready yet reluctant to resume the fight.

"Come with us and renounce your allegiance. If you refuse, we have the right to execute you on the spot," the heavier guard said.

"I doubt they'll comply, Neff," the thinner guard said, "Let's kill 'em now."

Neff, the heavier guard, rushed at the pair. Kol crouched, ready for the man, his rusted weapon ready.

Phetrix waved his hands again, using spells he hadn't touched in years. It was a risk to perform them out in the open like this. If the Seekers found him, they'd be on him quickly. With these two guards, he'd have to make sure they never made it back to Mortas. Then he'd have to find the dark man.

"Stand aside, Kol!"

Phetrix released a bolt of fire that struck the thin

guard.

Neff stumbled as he watched his partner burn. "Kreen! No!"

Phetrix waved his hands and another streak of fire released from his hands and engulfed Neff. The large man screamed in agony.

"Hurry Kol, take one of their swords and finish them!"

Kol smashed into Kreen, knocking the burning man over, and wrestled his sword away. Once in his possession, Kol slammed the blade through the burning leather armor into the man, piercing his flesh and killing him instantly. He withdrew the sword and went after Neff.

The larger man fought against the flames, trying to pat them out.

Phetrix prepared another blast, but Kol stepped in his way as he was about to release it. Pushing his hands aside, he let it go above Kol's head, the flames streaking wildly above him.

Kol spun. "Watch it! You nearly—"

Neff struck at him with his sword, catching the man in the back, and making him fall to the ground from his weight. Kol struggled with the flaming man who seemed not to be bothered with the fire surrounding him. His flesh turned black and charred but he refused to stop.

Phetrix waved his hands again, ready to strike, but feared he'd catch Kol in the attack.

Neff struck Kol with his massive fists, blood bursting from his nose.

Releasing the flames, Phetrix waved his hands again and created another blast of air. He pushed it at

Neff and it knocked the man off Kol.

Working fast, Phetrix wove a spell of lightning and let it fly toward Neff. It struck his flaming chest and exploded his insides, creating a massive hole where the snowflake was once displayed.

Kol regained his footing, wiping off the blood from his nose on his pants. "You got what you deserved!"

Phetrix wove his hands again, and let a spell of healing settle on Kol. "This might not work the best. My skill in healing was never great."

He watched as Kol registered the magic flowing over him. He could see in the man's eyes that it was working, though he didn't know how well.

When he was done, Phetrix scolded the man. "Don't ever do that again! What if a Seeker had found me? What if that wicked Rhoden had discovered me? We have to be more selective in how we handle them! At least until we get the heirs back. The dark man escaped. He'll be on the road in a hurry spreading word about us. We have to move. Once he alerts Mortas that I'm alive, he will flood the area with Seekers. We'll never be able to move without threat of being seen."

Kol shook his head. "I know. But the time has come! You saw what happened at the camp yesterday. If those two had anything to do with it, we did a great thing. Even if they didn't, they earned it for who they follow." He took the sword, removed the scabbard from Kreen, and put it on his waist. Leaving the old one behind.

"Let's move. The farm is nearby. We'll be free of this soon and be in a world where my spells might not even work. I don't know exactly, but it's our only chance of making things right again." Phetrix marched off, knowing Kol was following. The man might not be the smartest, but it was good to have a companion. Where they were going, he'd need all the help he could get.

CHAPTER

Thirty-Seven

DeWayne flew down the side streets and turned on the main road that would lead back to where he first picked the strange group up. He wanted to ask about his payment, but after witnessing what he had, thought it best to keep his mouth shut.

He glanced at Rhoden and spotted the finger sticking straight up. The site made him gag. He fought down the nausea, just wanting this nightmare to be over. The man mumbled something to himself, but he didn't want to look, fearing he'd see something far worse than a dislocated finger.

The girls were eerily silent considering their predicament. He looked in the rearview mirror and saw both of them staring straight ahead with blank looks as if drugged. A blue light reflected in the mirror. The cops had found them. He still had several miles to go before reaching their destination. "The police are following us."

Rhoden and Mortas swiveled in their seats to look behind.

Rhoden asked, "How much further?"

He accelerated. "Less than two miles." The look showed he didn't understand miles. "We're close."

The flashing lights gained on them. DeWayne could see more than one car pursued them. He swung around the corner, now blocks from his goal. The turn was at such a high speed, he could not hold the line. The van swerved, threatening to tip and roll. It bounced over a curb lifting everyone off their seats. He sideswiped the front of a brick building, sending sparks flying, before righting and driving down the sidewalk.

At the end of the block he veered into the street. With one block to go, the cops made the turn. They closed in fast.

DeWayne hit the brakes hard. With no one wearing a seat belt, everyone flew forward. Rhoden caught his weight by bracing his good hand on the dashboard, but his knees made contact and he cried out. Both girls ended up headfirst in the space between the two front seats. The bodyguard struck the seat in front of him head first, but Mortas appeared to hover above his seat.

"Hurry. Get out. They're right on top of us," DeWayne shouted.

The doors flew open all at once. Mortas glided out and faced the onrushing cars. Rhoden and the bodyguard pulled the zombie-like girls from the car and guided them toward where ever they were going. DeWayne watched in fascination, his fear subsided for the moment.

While Rhoden made strange hand gestures at the night air, the police screeched to a stop and multiple doors swung open. Shouts rained down on them. Everyone screamed for them to drop whatever weapons they possessed and lay down on the ground.

To Dewayne's amazement, the sky ripped apart. A long tear appeared like Rhoden had sliced through a canvas with a box cutter. He motioned to the bodyguard, who in robotic fashion tossed a girl over each shoulder and stepped toward the tear in the air.

The cops went ballistic in their commands and several broke cover from their cars and rushed forward. Rhoden, with his recovered amulet in hand, shoved his arm out like punching the air and the two cops flew backward. The other cops watched their comrades rolling along the ground in stunned silence. Then, as if an unseen director shouted 'action,' all hell broke loose.

Gunshots erupted and bullets filled the air. Rhoden made more hand movements. Whatever he did, the bullets missed him. Mortas grunted, and glanced at his arm where a stream of blood rolled down his sleeve. He gave it a look of curiosity, then a dark cloud shrouded his face. He shouted something in a voice straight from hell and flung his arms forward.

The first police car lifted off the ground and was flung hood over trunk through the air, landing on top of the second car, smashing both. One of the police opened up with a shotgun. Rhoden backed up, his features strained with effort.

The bodyguard stuffed each girl through the tear. They disappeared from sight. He stood to the side as Rhoden climbed through, then waited for Mortas. With a one armed sweep, two more police cars went sailing sideways, crashing to the ground twenty feet away. He turned, appeared to levitate, then was gone. Before the bodyguard could step through, a barrage of bullets slammed into him. He dropped to his knees, held for a second, then fell forward onto his face.

DeWayne could not believe his eyes. His fear was

so intense, thoughts were too difficult to form. His body vibrated with a violence that rocked the van. It wasn't the noise that shook him from his fugue, but the deafening silence.

The police approached with extreme caution. A face appeared to hang in the air suspended by some unseen force. Mortas glared at the cops. His eyes burned with a fire so intense, DeWayne imagined he felt the heat. The head swung in his direction and the eyes flared.

He screamed, ripped the stick into drive and jammed the pedal down. He was still screaming minutes later when he pulled to a stop, three blocks from his apartment building. He slumped in the seat, eyes still wide with fear and the scream fading like the end of a song track. He became aware of a warm wetness on his seat. At first he feared he'd been shot, then realized his bladder had released at some time during the ordeal.

With a glance at the mirror he discovered the rear window had been shattered at some point, too. His body was racked with a series of violent spastic convulsions. He had a strong urge to curl into a fetal position and suck on his thumb. His mind walked a narrow line between saneness and insanity. Part of his brain wanted to replay what he'd seen, but the other part fought to keep the scene hidden. Then, a new thought came to him. He helped madmen kidnap two girls, watched them kill a man, saw another two die, and was in the middle of a shootout with police—all that and he never got paid. The idea was enough to make him weep.

DeWayne had no idea how long he sat staring blankly, but somewhere, deep in his consciousness, the thought broke to the surface that he had to get up and out before the police found the car. As he sat up, he felt something stuck to his cheek. He brushed it off and it bounced on the seat. It caught his eyes and he gasped. It was a gold coin. He snatched it up and stared open-mouthed. He glanced down and found two more coins and something else—a stone of some sort that looked like a gem he'd never seen before. Not that he had much experience with gems of any kind. He held it eye level and stared mesmerized. It winked at him. A smile spread across his face.

He attempted to wipe the car down, but decided it wasn't worth the trouble. He left the keys in the ignition. It would be gone by morning. He zombie-walked home, praying he never saw Rhoden or, that crazed demon from hell boss of his ever again. Then, he focused on the gold coins and adapted his prayer to at least not for a while.

CHAPTER

Thirty-Eight

Marvin Grant left his favorite after-work hang out, a cop bar called Fuzzy's. As a bachelor, most nights he ate dinner there and some nights imbibed a few more drinks then he should. Tonight was one of those nights. Though not drunk, at least to his definition, he might struggle to pass a field sobriety test.

He slipped into the car and started the engine. As he was buckling his seat belt the radio squawked requesting all available units and announcing a homicide and chase. He noted the location of the chase as the various cars answered the call and took up pursuit. It wasn't far from where he was at the moment. Although he wouldn't get involved since he'd been drinking, he decided to follow in case of an emergency.

He pulled Vega's Tic Tacs from the console and popped four, then did a u-turn away from the curb and headed in the direction of the chase. He drove fast, but not at pursuit speed. Ahead, a car raced past. He guessed it was the suspects vehicle. By the time he got to the corner, four squad cars whizzed past. He let them go, then made the turn. He didn't want to add his lights to the color display unless necessary, so he followed at a distance.

The squad car's brake lights flashed on in unison. Officers leaped from barely stopped vehicles. He pulled to the side of the road a quarter of a block away. The sound of gunshots echoed off the buildings. Grant unbuckled his seat belt, slid his service weapon from the holster and opened the door.

He had just placed a foot on the street when a squad car lifted into the air and crashed atop another one.

"What the hell was that?" he said, ducking to avoid stray bullets and other flying vehicles. He jogged to the sidewalk and crept closer, using parked cars for cover.

A police officer went flying through the air and smashed into a building. He hit hard and slid down the wall, landing in a sitting position before toppling over. More gunshots followed, including several shotgun blasts. Grant moved to where he had an angle for a shot. He didn't want to discharge his weapon especially having been drinking, but his brothers were in trouble. He took aim at a man who appeared to hover above the ground. He was so astonished by the sight he held his fire until the man disappeared into thin air.

A second man levitated off the ground. Grant took aim, but before he could pull the trigger, the two remaining squad cars skidded sideways, colliding with each other. The officers scattered to avoid being crushed. The second man disappeared, leaving the biggest man alone. He reached up to what looked like a tear in the air. A hand reached out of, what? To help the man up. Grant could not let the man escape and his fellow policemen were no condition to stop him.

He aimed his weapon, a gun he'd never fired outside the shooting range, and pulled the trigger three times. The body jerked, took a step and dropped to his knees. A face that floated in midair, sans torso or legs, glowered at him. Then with a sudden flash, was gone like some illusionist vanishing from a stage.

A car, the one that transported the disappearing men, raced away from the scene. Grant raised his gun, but the car was around the corner before he had a chance to sight. He stood and walked dumbfounded toward the fallen man. A few other policemen got up. They challenged him, ordering him to drop his gun, until he showed his badge. He stepped over the body of the man he shot, kicked away the gun lying next to him and bent to check for a pulse. He found none. Fifteen years on the job and the first time he had to use his weapon he killed a man.

There would be all kinds of investigations, not only into the events that transpired before they got here, but also with all the bizarre things he'd witnessed, along with the shooting. If he feared being busted for drinking, the things he witnessed had long ago shocked him sober. He holstered his gun and went to assist the injured. It was going to be a long night.

CHAPTER

Thirty-Nine

It took two days for Phetrix and Kol to reach the farm. He'd not been there before, but Samuel's instructions were clear. The farm looked exactly like how he described it in his journal, all the way down to the dark orange color of the barn.

"Phetrix, are you sure about this? What you say sounds unreal."

"Kol, I know it can be difficult to understand, but I swear to you it's real. I've seen it. I've been there once. The heirs are there. By now they should be . . . eighteen years old? If I'm figuring things correctly that is."

Kol shook his head. "It's too much to grasp."

"You'll see. And then . . . we'll have work to do."

They marched through tall grass and headed for the northwest edge of the farm where a boulder jutted from the ground.

Kol seemed nervous, maybe even worried about what was to come.

"Phetrix, why don't we just connect with the rebels and fight Mortas? With your powers, surely we could cause damage."

"Without the heirs, it's meaningless. The prophecy—"

"Don't tell me you believe those old stories?"

Phetrix stopped and regarded the man.

"Of course I do. It's why I've done everything I

have. It's the *only* reason I still breath. Have these past years not proven how true they are?"

"These years have proven how inept Mortas is. It proves how corrupt a man he is, but it doesn't prove the prophecies are true."

Phetrix shook his head. "Then stay here. Go fight your meaningless battle and lose your life for nothing. I choose to fulfill the prophecy and bring back the heirs. Only once they return can we defeat Mortas and restore the land. Believe me or not. Help me or stay. No matter your decision, I will continue on to fulfill my duty."

Kol waved him off. "I have no connections here. If you believe so strongly, I should at least hang around to see if it happens. What's the difference between a fight here or a fight at this other place you say exists?"

Phetrix smiled at the man. He had a point.

"I promise you won't be disappointed by the strange world we're about to enter. It's like nothing you've ever seen."

The late afternoon sun hung in a blue sky streaked with clouds. It was a cool day and the birds in the far off trees sung softly. For Phetrix, it was an ideal afternoon. What he was about to try would change the world he knew forever. He'd either succeed in his quest, or he and Kol would die in a foreign land as defeated foes. He stopped and closed his eyes listening to the birds. He might never make it back here and he wanted a memory to cling to.

"Are you alright? What's wrong?"

"Nothing at all. I wanted to grasp Chevalon one last time, just in case."

Kol shielded his eyes and scanned the fields around them. "A farm. Your last memory might be a farm. Too bad it wasn't a tavern or something with a bit more atmosphere." He smiled and clapped Phetrix on the back.

They moved closer to the boulder. "This is the place. Are you ready Kol?"

"No. But don't let that stop you."

Phetrix closed his eyes and swirled his hands in the air, remembering the motions he used many years ago to open the seam while in the castle. At first, nothing moved. The air was still and the birds went silent. Then, with a loud crack and a bright flash, a line of light emerged. It stood taller than either of the men. It shimmered and then expanded, opening wider.

"By the gods," Kol said softly. "What is that place?"

Phetrix opened his eyes to see a bustling city with buildings much larger than anything he'd ever seen in Chevalon. Wheeled chariots raced across streets that were smoother and cleaner than those within their cities.

"What is that place?"

"It's a strange world, unlike ours. There are more people than you can imagine. The heirs are hidden there."

"What's the name of the place?"

Phetrix smiled, recalling the name scrawled in Samuel's journal. "That place is called Chicago."

Phetrix released his spell and the seam wavered, but held strong. "We need to go through. Stay close to me once we do. I've been there once and it can be overwhelming. We'll need to find different clothes quickly. We won't fit in looking like we do."

"Yeah, sure," Kol replied absently. His eyes were fixed on the scene showing through the seam.

"Shall we?" Phetrix stepped into the seam and his foot set down on a hard surface made of what looked to be stone but was wider and flatter then any he'd known. He turned around and Kol was still on the other side of the seam.

"Kol, come on! It won't stay open for long."

The man looked like he was about to flee.

"Hurry Kol! It's the only way!"

Kol sighed and closed his eyes, mumbling something Phetrix couldn't hear. Then he looked through the seam at Phetrix.

"I'm ready."

Kol walked forward, but the seam started to shrink and narrow.

"Oh no! Kol, the seam is closing! Run! Get through before it closes!"

Kol ran and tripped over something in the grass.

"Kol!"

Fortunately, he landed on the other side of the seam moments before it sealed shut.

He made it.

CHAPTER

Forty

Samuel slowed the car at the cross road, peering down the street to the house where Princess Elysande and her guardians had been living. Police cars and emergency vehicles swarmed the area. Their street was blocked by the mass of vehicles. He had no way of getting inside to discover the amount of destruction and death that had occurred.

Two men guided a gurney down the front walk toward a waiting ambulance. The body was not observable, being inside a black bag. Judging by the mound the body inside created, the deceased was quite large. He thought of Markus, the guardian he had coerced initially into protecting the princess, and prayed he wasn't the victim.

Two men in suits stepped out onto the front porch. One was short, stocky and black. The second man might have been the first's brother, in physique and mannerism, except for the skin color. They spoke and the black man glanced back inside the house, while his partner shook his head and dragged a hand over his head. Samuel took the gestures to mean, whatever happened inside had been either inexplicable or grotesque, maybe both.

They stepped aside, to allow a second gurney to descend, this one also carrying a bagged body of an approximate size as the first. His fear grew. Markus may not have survived the encounter with whoever came calling. Were the assailants from this world or the other? He wasn't sure why he held onto that hope—that it might have been a break-in gone bad. In his heart, he knew the truth. The princess had been discovered. The only question left was whether she was there when the attack occurred or elsewhere. He had to find Alyanna, the other guardian.

As if on cue, she was led out by a male and female EMT. Samuel let out a long breath of relief. But if she was here, where was the princess? She was never supposed to be out of their sight, even if the girl was not aware of their scrutiny. Did that mean she'd been here? For once, he prayed they had allowed the girl to go out unprotected. He studied Alyanna. She looked shaken and leaned on the EMT's for support, but otherwise appeared uninjured. Her head hung as if incapable of holding it erect. Perhaps it was from the knowledge she failed to keep her charge protected.

The black detective stopped them for a moment, said something, then motioned for a uniformed officer to accompany them. They climbed into the back of a waiting ambulance. Minutes later, the EMS vehicle drove off. Samuel followed. He had to speak with Alyanna. He had to know what he was dealing with.

He parked in the hospital lot and watched as Alyanna was placed in a wheelchair and taken inside the emergency room entry. The cop followed close behind. Samuel worked up a plan and exited the car. He rushed through the doors in time to see Alyanna wheeled through double doors at the rear of the room. He went that way to catch them, but a nurse stepped in front of him.

"Can I help you, sir?"

"Ah, they just brought my niece in. I was trying to catch them."

"She's being taken for examination. If you want to sit in the waiting room, someone will let you know when she's through."

"But . . ."

"Sir, there's nothing you can do for the moment. You are not allowed back there right now. Please, take a seat." She pointed behind him to the rows of mismatched seats and gave him a look, that said, 'Don't challenge me.'

His shoulders slumped. He turned and walked, glancing over his shoulder. The nurse had been expecting something and stood with arms folded and an 'I dare you,' look. He sat.

More than two hours later, the nurse came over and said, "Your niece has been taken to a room. They're keeping her for further evaluation. She is in room three twenty-two. You may not be able to see her yet, but you can check in at the nurses station and wait upstairs."

"Thank you."

Samuel found the elevators and rode to the third floor. He ignored the nurse's station and hunted for the room. He didn't have to look hard. The cop stood guard outside her door. He hesitated, then proceeded. It was perfectly normal for a relative to be here and want to see the patient.

He nodded at the cop and turned to the door. The man extended an arm to block his path. His other hand slid to his weapon. "I'm sorry, sir, No visitors."

"But, I'm her uncle."

"I understand, sir. But for the moment she is off limits to everyone including family until the detectives can speak with her."

"This is outrageous. She's my niece and I want to see her."

"I understand, sir, but no matter who you are, I'm not letting you in. You need to lower your voice and go sit down in the waiting room. Someone will inform you when she can have visitors."

Samuel stood gaping at the man, not sure what to do next. He could get into the room with ease if he wanted, and he did. With a glance up and down the hall, he quickly formed a plan. He went to the waiting room, found a red plastic chair and carried it back. The cop stiffened when he saw him approach.

"Sir, you don't want to make this a problem."

"Not at all."

He set the chair down against the wall next to the door.

"You can't sit here, either."

"The chair's not for me."

The officer's brows knitted. "Who's it for?"

"You." Samuel smiled.

Whatever the cop saw in that smile caused him to reach for his weapon. Samuel mumbled a few words, waved his hand in front of the man's face as the gun slid from the holster, but before he could bring it up, his head lulled to the side. Samuel caught the man before he collapsed and dragged him to the chair. He sat him down, then holstered the gun. With another quick glance down the halls. He entered the room.

CHAPTER

Forty-One

He closed the door and stood studying the woman in the bed. He wanted to feel compassion, to comfort her agony, but the princess might be in danger and this woman was to blame. She cried softly, unaware of his presence. He stepped closer to her until she noticed. Her head turned. Within seconds of recognizing him, she burst into tears. He advanced to calm her. Sobs racked her body. The heart rate rose, the intervals between beeps decreased.

"Oh Samuel," she extended a hand to him. He let it hang, angry with her failure. "They have her."

"Who has her?" his tone harsh.

She pulled her hand back. "The mage came for her. They killed Markus," she screamed his name.

He stepped to her bed and glared at her. She cringed and withdrew to the far side, wincing from the effort. The pain made her gasp. She clutched at her side. A red welt stretched across her face. Her chest was bandaged, perhaps indicating broken ribs. She had at least put up a fight.

Samuel allowed some of the anger to drain. She would have been no match for Rhoden. Their best hope of defense had always been not being discovered. He trained the guardians as best he could, but in the end, it was never going to be enough. He blew out a breath allowing the hostility to go with it.

"Tell me, Alyanna. What happened?"

She explained adding how she killed one of the bodyguards. But once Rhoden entered, he incapacitated her. Unfortunately, she had been rendered unconscious and never saw what happened to the Princess. Had Rhoden managed to escape with her or was he still in this world? He needed to go. To plan for either contingency.

"You did the best you could, Alyanna. Rest. Get well." He turned to go.

"Samuel, Markus is dead."

He didn't respond, nor did he look at her.

"We gave up everything for you. Our homes, our futures. Our lives."

He spun now, anger driving his words. "You gave up nothing. You would have been killed or enslaved had you stayed. I gave you a life, a future. Am I upset Markus is dead?" He paused, his voice softened. "Yes. But I have to find the princess. If I succeed, there will be time to mourn him later. If I don't, it won't matter since I will have joined him." He opened the door. "Be well, Alyanna."

***

Margaret Sterling walked out of the conference room and down the hall toward the lab. She just finished yet another long explanation of what happened the day of the so-called fire. Still no cause had been determined, but fortunately, neither had any damage. She was tired, not just physically drained, but mentally exhausted and fed up with having to explain her actions.

It wasn't her fault some old geezer got into the lab. *She* certainly didn't admit him.

She made a turn and ran into a man.

"Oh, excuse me," she said stepping away.

"My fault entirely," the older man said. "Pardon me."

He moved away from her down the opposite direction. Clearly something pressing was on his mind. She made it two more steps before a nagging in a far corner of her brain slowed her steps. She was brought to a halt three steps later as the nagging notion took root and fought to the surface. Five seconds later she had it and whirled to give pursuit. She raced through the door dodging past incoming and outgoing patients and finally stood out front scanning the parking lot.

"No, I'm not letting you get away this time," she muttered, determined. Still, not finding him, she pulled out her cell phone and dialed the number of the detective who'd given it to her. She expected it to go to voicemail, but to her surprise was answered on the third ring.

"Grant."

"Detective, I don't know if you'll remember me, but this is Margaret Sterling from City Hospital."

"Sure, Ms. Sterling. I remember. what can I do for you?"

"That man came back. The one who was in the lab the day of the fire. I just saw him leaving."

"Can you see him now?"

"No, but he only just left."

"I'm close. Where are you?"

"Out front."

"Wait there."

***

Samuel sat in the car contemplating his next move. He took out the cell phone from a jacket pocket and stared at it for a moment. Such a strange item. Had he not been forced to live in this world for all these years, he never in his wildest dreams would have thought of such a thing.

He typed in a number from memory. Dina answered on the first ring.

"Tell me you still have the prince."

"Yes. Why?" A note of panic crept into her voice. "What's happened?"

"They found and took the princess."

"Oh no. Did they cross back with her?"

"Unknown. I'm going to find out, but I need you to put the emergency plan into effect. I can not be sure they have not discovered you, too. Go to the safe house, use the security I showed you. If you do not hear back from me. You are on your own."

"Understood." She hesitated and he could hear in the silence she had something more to say. "Speak, Dina."

"Don't you think it is about time the prince knew the truth?"

"If I do not come back, use your best judgment as to what you do or what you tell the prince." He was about to disconnect when he changed his mind. "No, get him out of town now and then tell him. Tell him everything, then increase his training. It will be better if he is involved in his own defense."

"Samuel."
"Yes?"
"Good luck."

He disconnected. If Rhoden had already secreted the princess through the seam, he would need a lot more than luck. He drove out of the lot as a police car approached, lights flashing, siren wailing. He braked, let the unmarked car pass, then drove on.

CHAPTER

Forty-Two

Grant screeched the car to a stop in front of Margaret Sterling as she waved her arms frantically over her head. He hopped out of the car and ran to her.

She ran to meet him, pointing toward the street. "You just missed him. He just left the lot. He turned left."

"Did you notice the type of car?"

"It was a green four door. I think a Buick. You should still be able to catch him."

Grant didn't reply. He whirled back into the car and sped away. Once he reached the street he lit the light and made the turn. The green car was not in sight. He doubted success, but after the night he'd had already, he needed a win. Ten minutes later, he pulled to the side of the road and pounded the steering wheel.

***

Samuel made a stop at his apartment and gathered the items he had both saved and collected should he ever have need to cross through the seam again. In truth, he'd been back several times, to keep in contact with those still loyal to the crown, but none of those trips required him to do what this journey called for.

He was getting older and was sorely out of practice.

He wondered if he still had the ability to deal with this threat or if his time had finally come to an end.

The car nosed up the ramp of the parking garage. He parked on the fourth of six levels, to the far right. He stripped out of his suit and shoes and replaced them with his robes and boots. The clothes and other items of this world were locked in the trunk.

***

Grant made a U-turn, frustrated and thinking about going back to Fuzzy's. He no longer wanted to face sleep sober. He debated going back to the hospital, deciding instead to report his failure to Margaret Sterling by phone. At a stop light, he slid the phone from his pocket and glanced down to find the number. When he looked up, a green car had made the turn on the road out in front of him. It could be the same car, but it was going in the opposite direction. Still, wanting something to go right today, he decided to follow. He put the phone down on the passenger seat and turned on lights and sirens. He was the third car in line and had to wait for the cars in front of him to move to give him the room to go around them in the oncoming lane. The maneuver cost him several precious seconds. It took him a moment to find and lock on the green sedan, then it was all out pursuit.

He cut the distance in half and spotted the green car turning into a parking garage.

***

Samuel strode to the partial wall. This was the tricky part. The top half was open and he now faced a twenty-story office building. Normally he would wait until dark, but he could not afford to delay. If the princess had been taken, he had to get to her as fast as possible before that monster, Mortas got a chance to play with her and create a royal minion that would sway the people to give up the rebellion.

He dared not enter through the original seam, knowing Rhoden would have an ambush waiting for him. Through the years he'd searched for another path across. It had taken a long time and cost a lot of energy and strain on his brain and heart. There had been two false paths, one leading to a desolate world of harsh winds and torrid heat, the other an icy world so bone chilling his face numbed just peering through the seam.

However, he did find an alternate route, six of this world's miles from the original entry point. He used it once. The only other person with knowledge of the seam was Phetrix and an old man who lived on a farm not far from where he would enter. That man was his conduit to the rebels loyal to the king and queen.

As he took one long last look around the garage and the world he could see beyond, he heard from somewhere on one of the lower levels a car was coming fast, the tires squealing in protest. He then began the spell that could lead to his death. As the seam opened, his gaze rested on a window seven floors from the ground in the office building. A woman stood watching him, a mug of something in her hand.

She waved at him, evidently thinking his gesticulations were the like. He gave her a quick wave, stepped up onto the concrete wall, and stepped out into open air. His last sight of this world was the woman's horrified face, perhaps thinking he was about to commit suicide. As the seam closed behind him, he wondered what she thought now.

Grant found the car on the fourth level. He'd entered sans lights and siren, not wanting to spook the driver. He braked and scanned the garage, but the man was nowhere in sight. Had he changed cars and escaped past him? No, he didn't remember a car going the opposite direction. The only other choice was if he went up. Two more floors lay above.

He started moving and then slammed the brakes fast as he caught sight of the man standing on the edge of the half wall.

"Oh, don't tell me he's gonna jump." He slipped the stick into park and got out, mumbling "can this day get any stranger?"

As he ran the man waved to someone in one of the office buildings. He didn't have the angle yet to see who. In front of him, just beyond the wall, trees appeared, then he saw a what looked like a very old barn. They appeared out of nowhere and seemed to float in the air. What the hell was going on?

Grant ran around the green car and toward the man who looked oblivious to his presence. The man calmly stepped off the ledge. Grant screamed, "No!" But he was too late. The man was gone. He reached the wall and looked down. No body was in sight. He leaned further for a better angle. Nothing. Where did he go? he looked out straight off the wall looking for the tree and barn, but they had disappeared as well.

"I'm losing my mind."

He glanced up and spotted a woman pressed against the glass of the building across and above him. He lifted his arms in a shrug. She shook her head and returned the shrug. Now he regretted asking if the day could get any stranger. It just had.

He climbed back in his car and sat wondering what to do. A car came up behind him and honked. he wasn't ready to move so motioned him around. He sat in the car running through the events of the day. The flying cars, the disappearing men. Now this guy vanished. Had aliens come to the planet?

Finally, he decided to go down and check the sidewalk to verify the man had not plunged to his death. As he drove away a shouted voice caught his attention. Grant hit the brakes and looked for the source. In the rear view mirror, two men came into view in the same place the other man had disappeared. Both were dressed in shabby clothes and looked like homeless men. What caught his attention though was the sword one man carried.

"Oh hell no. This can't be happening."

He exited the car and stared over the roof at the two men. His first thought was he needed a drink. His next was this was going to be a long night.

ACKNOWLEDGEMENTS

Thanks

This was an interesting project for me. I'd never co-written a story before, but I have to say I couldn't have had a better partner than Jason. The story was fun to write to conceptualize. I'm looking forward to the second book in the series. I want to thank Jason for agreeing to undertake this project.

I'd also like to thank author and editor Steve Wilhelm for agreeing to step in last minute to help us complete the book and have it ready by our deadline. Well done, Steve.

As always, a special shout out to all those who have stuck with me over the years. It's been a fun journey and promises to only get better. Thanks for your continued support. Read all you want. I'll write more.

-Ray

To say this was interesting is an understatement. As it is the first co-written project I've done, it's been a blast. I can't say enough great things about Ray and his direction with this.

Thanks to Steve for the edits and MIBL Art for the rocking cover!

The next books are gonna be great! We've got all kinds of amazing things in store. Thanks for reading.

-Jason

ABOUT THE AUTHORS

Ray Wenck

Ray Wenck is a retired teacher and prior owner of DeSimone's Italian restaurant. He is the author of the *Danny Roth* thriller series and the highly acclaimed, post-apocalyptic series, *Random Survival*.

The *Danny Roth* series includes *Teammates, Teamwork, Home Team* and *Stealing Home* and *Group Therapy*.

The Random Survival series includes The Long Search For Home, The Endless Hunt and A Trip to Normal.

Also published are the humorous YA adventure, *Warriors of the Court*, the paranormal thriller, *Ghost of a Chance.* the suspense thriller, *Live To Die Again* and the Zombie thrillers, *Tower of the Dead* and *Island of the Dead*. His latest release is *Pick-A-Path: Apocalypse*, a choose your own adventure for adults.

When not writing Ray hikes, cooks and plays harmonica with whatever band will let him sit in.

Other titles by Ray Wenck

The Danny Roth Mystery/Suspense Series

Teammates
Teamwork
Home Team
Stealing Home
Group Therapy
Double Play

Random Survival Post-Apocalyptic Series

Random Survival
The Long Search For Home
The Endless Struggle
Hanging On
Book 5 currently untitled (coming soon)

The Dead Series

Tower of the Dead
Island of the Dead
Escape the Dead

Stand Alone Titles

Warriors of the Court – young adult fantasy
Live To Die Again – suspense thriller
Ghost of a Chance – Paranormal
Pick-A-Path: Apocalypse – Book 1
Pick-A-Path: Apocalypse – Book 2
Super Me
The Con

available @ raywenck.com

ABOUT THE AUTHORS

Jason J. Nugent

Jason J. Nugent has been a paperboy, pizza maker, dishwasher, restaurant manager, promotional products sales rep, chamber of commerce director, and one time BBQ champion. He has skated with Tony Hawk, had a babysitter with a serial killer brother, and is followed by rapper Chuck D on Twitter. He and his wife share a home in beautiful Southern Illinois with their son, two cats, and two dogs.

He's the author of the thrilling young adult scifi series *The Forgotten Chronicles: The Selection, Rise of the Forgotten, The War for Truth* and two collections of horror / dark fiction short stories: *(Almost) Average Anthology* and *Moments of Darkness*.

More information, his blog, and a monthly newsletter sign-up can be found at jasonjnugent.com.

Made in United States
North Haven, CT
14 November 2024